I0642749

ADVENTURES OF
BOZO &
CHICK

Ranjit Lal has written over thirty books for both adults and children. Some of his books include *The Crow Chronicles, The Life and Times of Altu-Faltu, Bossman* and the *Kala Shaitan, Birds from My Window*. He has been a winner of the Crossword Best Children's Book Award for *Faces in the Water* and *Our Nana was a Nutcase*.

ADVENTURES OF
BOZO &
CHICK

Terror at Bedlam House

RANJIT LAL

RED TURTLE
RUPA

Published in Red Turtle by
Rupa Publications India Pvt. Ltd 2018
7/16, Ansari Road, Daryaganj
New Delhi 110002

Sales centres:

Allahabad Bengaluru Chennai
Hyderabad Jaipur Kathmandu
Kolkata Mumbai

Copyright © Ranjit Lal 2018

This is a work of fiction. Names, characters, places and incidents are either the product of the author's imagination or are used fictitiously and any resemblance to any actual person, living or dead, events or locales is entirely coincidental.

All rights reserved.
No part of this publication may be reproduced, transmitted, or stored in a retrieval system, in any form or by any means, electronic, mechanical, photocopying, recording or otherwise, without the prior permission of the publisher.

ISBN: 978-93-5304-138-0

First impression 2018

10 9 8 7 6 5 4 3 2 1

The moral right of the author has been asserted.

This book is sold subject to the condition that it shall not, by way of trade or otherwise, be lent, resold, hired out, or otherwise circulated, without the publisher's prior consent, in any form of binding or cover other than that in which it is published.

For
all those who
shouldn't be afraid...

1

$\mathcal{B}$efore anything else, get this straight—you need to know this right in the beginning in order to understand what followed later.

I am a patriot and if anyone insults or threatens my country, I will take action. You know what I mean?

I am also very loyal to my friends and the people I trust and will help them no matter what the consequences.

Sometimes, as you will see, this can be a problem.

It makes me furious every time there's a terrorist attack on our country, and there have been too many—the worst being the attacks on Mumbai. Most of the time, it is said that terror strikes are due to 'intelligence failure'—because someone somewhere remained blind, deaf and dumb to vital clues and signals. We have to be ever-vigilant, and I've taken a solemn oath to be so. Last year, at Chandigarh station, while returning from Kasauli, I noticed an abandoned bag under a bench near the waiting room. I went up to the nearest cop and pointed it out to him. He rudely said, '*Kya makhaul kar raha hain* (Are you trying to be funny)?' He then picked it up and went off to catch the train that had just come. Really, if cops do stupid things like that and have that kind of attitude, what can you expect? If they had seen the boats carrying the terrorists sail into Mumbai, they would have just said, '*Haan, machchi walle honge* (Yes they must be fishermen)!' My credo is absolute vigilance at all times.

To that end, I've started learning a martial arts discipline (which one, I cannot divulge)—even if it is more for defence than offence. I'm going to be a COBRA commando when I'm old enough, though I think I'm old and mature enough even now. Lambu, a.k.a 'Chick', who lives next door says that I behave more like a wannabe mafia don, and calls me Bozo. I'm 15 and put myself through rigorous physical training every day. I'm a full five-feet-one-inch tall, solidly built with hefty biceps, and sport a GI's buzz-cut. Okay, so maybe Lambu is five-feet-four-inch tall and runs faster than I do—but she's 16 and has legs like a giraffe, so what can one do if god made her like that? 'Gangly' is the word for her—long legs, long arms, a long oval face and very long black hair in a single plait, swishing like an elephant's tail. Like I said, god made her like that.

We live in Dubash Mansions 'circa 1920' which Chick calls Bedlam House. It is owned by Dr V R Dubash MBBS etc etc. and his wife, Mridula Aunty, who are the landlords. It is a huge old oblong building in chrome yellow, like a block of butter. It has wide white verandahs running around it, that catch the sea breeze, and big green-shuttered windows. It is located right at the edge of a small town (I'm not telling you which, for security reasons), on top of a steep high plateau that overlooks the sea, not too far from Mumbai. The school bus turns and scuttles back to town after dropping us here. The house is surrounded by coconut and casaurina groves as well as chickoo and mango orchards. There are lots of other trees and fields growing rice and dals and wheat as well as vegetables, also owned by the Dubashes. Below it, at the bottom of a fifty-foot sheer cliff-face, is a wide curving beach, guarded at both ends (north and south) by steep and very sharp rocky cliffs and outcrops, making it virtually a private beach for us. We call the rocks the Black Diamond Rocks and the outcrops, the Lobsters' Pincers. We can get down to the beach via the steps carved into the cliff-face from the garden gate.

By 'we', I mean the following:

Myself—Rohan, and my younger brother, Sohail (he's 7 and a hell of a pain in the butt and thankfully doesn't play much of a part in what happened here); you don't need to know the surname, so that's enough. Suffice to say, I control the show around here, and run a tight ship at that, even though I was forced to call Chick 'didi' for many years, and sometimes even now.

Lambu, a.k.a Chick—the real name is Nitu and she lives next door. She's a whiz with computers and can be a real nosey parker.

Aslam, 14 and my wingman, lives above us and is keen on playing piano and keyboard which he's very good at, as well as the mouth organ, which he's not good at. He's still pretty pissed off that his upcoming piano exam made him miss nearly all the action that took place over these past days.

All our families or parts of families who also live with us, and whom you'll meet in a bit.

Dr Dubash, better known as Dr D, is a children's specialist—a pediatrician I think they're called—a big bald fellow with a bellow and booming laugh. He's one heck of a joker and is forever going on about me and Chick, just because we've lived here and played together since we were naked babies. Much to our annoyance, he keeps singing this ancient number by some fossilized dude named Cliff Richard, called 'The Young Ones,' when we're around. Listen to it on YouTube and you'll know what I mean. His wife, Mridula Aunty, is something else. If I was the marrying kind (and I can't be if I want to be a COBRA commando), I'd like to marry someone like her. She's small and slim ('petite', Chick says), and curly-haired. She speaks softly, but, man, she can put diamond cutters into that soft golden syrupy voice of hers when she wants to. Often, she needs to—she's a dog trainer, you see, and her clients include the cops' canine squad. Training classes are held from Monday to Saturday, in the morning and evening, and often on Sundays too. She's good at her job considering the number of people who drive their pooches all the way out here every day for training sessions. She also does house calls if necessary. The Dubashes are our godparents too.

'Don't you see?' Chick once told me, grabbing me by the shoulder and pointing, as we watched a training session. 'It's not the dogs aunty is training—it's their stupid owners and handlers, even the cops! And they don't even realize it!' Actually, I didn't believe that. I thought the cops and owners allowed themselves to be 'trained' just because Mridula Aunty was such a pretty lady— anybody would. Really, I wouldn't mind being 'trained' by her. Pity, I didn't have a dog.

'Maybe you should join them,' I told her sarcastically, 'considering your stupid Cushion must be the wildest dog in town. You should call her Cactus, not Cushion. She's always scratching and nipping and snapping.'

'She is not and does not. And don't call her Cactus. She's a pedigreed Yorkie!'

That leads us to the incident from where the name 'Bedlam House' came. Every evening, we'd return from school and battle our way through the lobby—past bawling brats and barking dogs and freaked-out adults, trying to control both. It really was bedlam in the lobby every evening. 'Ground Zero' of the building was occupied by Dr D's clinic and Mridula Aunty's office, the waiting rooms and a training hall. There were two waiting rooms, one for the children only and the other for dogs and their owners, including the children.

'You see, sometimes it's good for the children to wait with the dogs—the animals calm them down,' Mridula Aunty told us.

She added with a smile, 'It's up to their parents to decide that, though sometimes I think those children need to see me more than Uncle!'

Mridula Aunty also runs an NGO in the nearby town, which according to Chick, helps women who have 'problems' with their husbands and boyfriends (like when they get drunk or try to set them on fire or throw acid on them or beat them), which she wants to join too, once she's done with school. Lambu's eyes glint like a hunting leopard's when she starts talking about this and you gotta be careful of what you say to her—Chick can just flare up like firework in response to the most innocuous remark. Sometimes, of course, I deliberately needle her, making sure I have an exit strategy because her long arms and legs can reach you from across the room in seconds. And I don't think it's right for a guy to get into physical combat with a chick—even if she seems to think otherwise.

The Dubashes live on the first floor of Bedlam House. The second floor has two spacious flats; one is ours and the identical one across the landing is occupied by Lambu and her parents. Upstairs, Aslam lives with his mother and baby sister Sarika, and their maid Amma in a single flat with a terrace, where we fly kites.

Mine and Lambu's dad are business buddies from way back and own a factory that makes highly technical engine and gearbox parts for cars. Aslam's dad is the captain of a gigantic oil tanker, ploughing its way through the world's oceans at any given time. Our moms do different things too. Chick's mom runs a string of 'boutique' shops in several places, including Mumbai, Goa, New Delhi and Bengaluru ('Ma really rips off those hoity-toity socialite mwah-mwah darling types,' she often says with a delicious shudder. 'But really, what a way to make a living!') Aslam's mom, quite a 'tiger mom', is a history professor in a college in Mumbai and hell-bent on Aslam getting a music scholarship abroad. As for mom, she is a high-up executive in a multinational advertising company in Mumbai. We don't see much of them during the week—Lambu's mom travels a lot, and they all share a small service flat in Mumbai where they often stay when work keeps them late, which is nearly every day. (It is almost a three-hour-long drive otherwise).

We've lived here since we were born and have spent umpteen nights with the Dubashes, who were like the 'constant north star' in our lives. They had no kids of their own, only this doofus Rottweiler called Night, so I guess, they didn't mind it at all. But it is quite mortifying to think that Dr D has seen us all in our birthday suits. He still gives us all our inoculations and vaccinations, and takes a ghoulish delight in doing so.

'He's wacko,' Chick would say, shaking her head. 'He makes all this *halla* (noise), sings and dances like a headhunter at a chop-chop party, and then you hardly feel the needle! After that, he grins and winks! Really!'

It can be embarrassing to live next door to the same chick all your life, ever since you were in diapers—especially if she's older than you. There are just too many things you can be blackmailed about; especially with home videos, which unfortunately, both Lambu's dad and Papa were crazy about. Every weekend, since we were little, if they were home, they'd have their handy-cams out. They would film our every move all day, which would be grandly screened for public consumption on birthdays—much to our horror—amidst much grown-up squealing and laughing. As for our moms, you will not believe what they've recently done!

Chick came running up to me one day, with her laptop, and her face scarlet.

'Bozo, check this out! Can you believe it? Our moms have

become Facebook freaks! They've all got Facebook accounts and have *hazar* (thousand) "friends". Now they're posting corny things we might have said when we were idiotic kids (and even now), or every little achievement or "cute" picture, only to be "liked" by scores of similar moronic moms who make these asinine, cutesy remarks and tell them how clever their little darlings are! It's so gross!'

She scrolled up and down a bit. 'Look at this! You remember this?'

I did. It was horrific. I must have been three years old for crying out loud and Chick was four. We were trundling down the beach together in our swimsuits; she was holding my hand. Then, suddenly, she stopped walking, threw her arms around me and smooched me smack on the mouth just like you see them doing it in the films you're not supposed to watch till you're 18 or something. In the background, we could hear peals of parental laughter and delight. Needless to add, the clip was titled 'Childhood Sweethearts'—or something corny like that.

'Sheesh, just what kind of films did your parents let you see, that made you do that?' I asked her in disgust.

'Bozo, it's got over 500 "likes". That means over 500 weirdos have seen this! How can I show my face to society again?'

'And what about me? Man, this has got to stop!'

This, apparently, was easier said than done. Lambu for all her computer whiz skills couldn't remove the posts and a direct appeal to our moms got this response: 'But, what's wrong with them? They're so sweet! And you are growing up so quickly!' That was followed by another horrific picture of both of us—probably a year and two years old at the time—being bathed together in the same enormous bucket and looking very happy about it. I tell you, babies are morons. Luckily, as we quickly grew and turned into wacko teens, the filming stopped. Though, every now and then, yet another ghastly Facebook post pops up, sent from one of our moms, lamenting how quickly their little darlings have grown up. Of course, it is always accompanied with a silly picture.

Let me give you an idea of the lay of the land where we live, because it is, well, very different from places most kids we know live, and often getting a mobile signal is tough. Across the driveway from Bedlam House, beyond the portico, is a large unkempt lawn at two levels. This is where the dog training classes are held and it ends at the cliff-edge, guarded by a green wooden fence and a guard of honour of whispering casuarinas and coconut trees. The lower level garden gradually slopes into a large pond at its northern end, called Lotus Lake. I still remember the day when Dr D and Mridula Aunty took us down to Lotus Lake, affixed bright orange floaters to our arms and legs, and took us into the water. We were still toddlers then. They absolutely insisted we learnt to swim there. 'If you want to live here, you have to know how to swim here; period. This pond and the ocean out there are all hungrily waiting to gobble you up!' Dr D declared. Our parents had no choice but to agree. After all, both Dr D and Mridula Aunty were crack swimmers. Once we had mastered the pond, they took us down to the sea—where it was actually easier to float because of the salt water. Very soon, all three of us were 'swimming like ducks'—in Mridula Aunty's words.

Just beyond Lotus Lake is the playground—complete with swings, slides and seesaws—painted bright red, blue and yellow, and a sandpit (overkill, one might think, with the beach just down the cliff!). There's a grey stone wall about eight feet high running along the sea-facing cliff-side of the playground to discourage us from climbing over and falling down. But there's a secret hole in this wall—concealed by a rock we've rolled in front of it—and a steep rocky path going down to the beach from it, straight into a big clump of spinifex. We don't use it because it is pretty risky—especially for kids like Sohail. A dense grove of peepul, banyan, bael, neem, mango, and of course casaurina trees screens the eastern boundary of the playground. Up in the wide-spreading branches of the biggest banyan tree is our tree house, impossible to spot from the ground unless you know it's there.

Chick says it was built by Dr D and his brothers when they were kids, and I think there's truth in what she says. Every six months or so, Dr D himself climbs up and inspects it, and replaces whichever wooden planks and ropes he thinks are rotting. It's got a wooden plank floor and walls of woven branches, with windows. Chick has brought a whole set of big comfy jungle-green cushions from her house and scattered them around. Access is via a rope-ladder, cleverly disguised as a creeper-vine. We simply pull it up when we're all upstairs and don't want anyone to follow, though if you're a good tree climber, you can get up without it. The tree house is the perfect snooper's perch, much like the crow's nest of a ship, and sometimes creaks and sways just as much. From the windows, you get a great view of the sea to the west and of the gaunt, brooding 'Annex' to the east, just across the path.

We believe that the Annex is haunted and stay away from it. It is a rather grim structure built out of the same Black Diamond rock, two storeys high, with verandahs running around it. It crouches in the middle of an overgrown wild garden where the grass can draw blood if you stride through it. Vivid orange and scarlet mushrooms sprout like magic on the deadwood lying hidden in the high grass during the rains. Gnarled old trees, all hunchbacked and twisted, whisper secretively around it. The windows and sliding doors opening out into the verandahs are always closed and thickly curtained so you can't peep inside. It has often happened that while playing in the tree house, we got the willies when we spotted what looked like movements behind the thickly curtained windows of the house. At dusk, we sometimes still see lights flickering and moving, as if from one room to another.

It is pretty creepy—for months, we saw nothing and then just as we summoned enough courage to enter and explore the overgrown garden and cottage, we saw the curtains shift slightly as if moved by a gentle breeze or a sly hand. Suddenly, the light also switched on. We fled. This continued for days, even weeks, before the apparitions vanished again. We even told Dr D about the mysterious movements and lights, thinking he would just laugh it off and tell us we were imagining things. But he nodded seriously, his grey eyes glimmering and his two gold teeth glinting.

'Ah, so you've seen them too...' he whispered, sending icy shivers down our spines. 'Yes, that is an unfortunate property, with an unfortunate history—it belongs to aunty and me of course, but... There have been....happenings....there...and we've just decided to give the place a wide berth. You kids should too. Stay away from it, children!'

We did, for years, until one day, at dusk, we saw the light switch on in one of the rooms and switch off in another. Chick suddenly challenged me to go up to the front door of the cottage and knock.

'You think you're this big special forces commando He-man superhero? So go and knock on the door and see who's there, Bozo!' she said. 'I challenge you! Only the ground floor, mind you. I don't want you to fall down the stairs or anything while running away.' She smiled sweetly and put her hands on her hips, waiting for my response.

'Okay sweetheart, no problem!' I said breezily, spitting out the blade of grass I had been chewing casually, even though my heart was racing. I raised my eyebrows sardonically. 'If anything happens, don't feel guilty, Chick, like for the rest of your life.'

'I won't,' she said, smiling again. 'Now go, Bozo! And don't "sweetheart" me!'

'Boss, seriously, are you going to do this?' Aslam asked, his eyes wide. He was petrified of the supernatural.

'Yeah kiddo, nothing to it! Listen…if anything…happens, you can have my collection of model aircraft, including the Sukhoi!'

'Thanks boss!'

'And take care of the pest—give me your word on that.'

'Sure boss.'

I gave Chick a meaningful look.

'Okay, Chick! Nice knowing you…' I paused. 'If…anything happens, you go and tell mom, right? Because you'll owe her and me that!'

She snorted explosively.

I climbed down from the tree house and crossed the path. At the gate of the Annex, I turned around and waved at the tree house, a gesture of final farewell. Then I put my hands in my pockets (to show I was *bindass* [badass]), and sauntered up the gravel driveway leading up to the front door. The high grass on either side of the narrow driveway leaned towards me, brushing against my legs in a soft whispery, paintbrush-like way. The lantana hedges surrounding the garden glimmered with pink and yellow flowers, over which fuzzy golden moths whirred silently. A magpie-robin uttered a harsh 'chrrrr' from somewhere in the garden and a pair of spotted owlets stared at me from a crooked old gulmohar tree. I walked up to the small porch, gulped, raised my hand and knocked on the ancient wooden front door. And then, for good measure, I rang the bell too.

A little later, I heard a shuffle behind the door and tensed. Suddenly I was blinded as the porch light was switched on. I blinked. A large jet black eye appeared at the spyhole, the white glimmering like a poached egg. Then the light went out. I heard the locks being unlatched, bolts being drawn, and as the door creaked open very slightly, a face peered out. Actually, it was just a pair of big black eyes, peering out of a slit; the forehead, nose, face and mouth was covered with dark shadowy cloth.

'Yes?' a soft husky voice enquired. 'What do you want?'

I shook my head dumbly.

'N...nothing, s....sorry to disturb!' I turned and walked back briskly, trying very hard not to break into a run because the other two—Aslam and Chick—had come down from the tree house and were watching with open mouths from the garden gate.

'There!' I told Chick, 'I told you—nothing to it!'

'Bozo there's someone there! Someone's living there! We better tell Dr D. Maybe that person has been living there for years and pretending to be a ghost! Maybe it's a murderer! He could have grabbed you!' But was there new respect in those leopardess eyes of hers and in her husky voice? I think so. Chick was impressed.

'Yeah, he could have,' I said laconically. 'But I told him, "Ho Man! I come in peace for all mankind!" No issues!'

Chick eyed me speculatively but said nothing. Like I said, she was impressed.

'Man, that was something!' Aslam said, stars in his eyes.

Dr D shook his head slowly when he heard our tale. 'Kids, don't ever go there again!' He looked at me. 'Son, you were very brave, but foolish. You've seen the ghost of the Annex and have come back alive! They say it's been haunting that house for over five hundred years. Sometimes it disappears for months, no one knows where; they say, it just swims out to the sea on full moon nights, strangles smugglers in their boats and then vanishes beneath the waves with their booty. And then it emerges again and spends time at the cottage... No one knows why.'

Mridula Aunty happened to overhear this and put her hands on her hips and shook her head exasperatedly.

'Darling, don't scare them like that—look at poor Sohail's face, and even Nitu is looking pale.' Then she smiled and sat us down.

'Dears, Uncle's been spinning you these yarns and talking nonsense for years now. The truth is that Uncle and I have been renting out the Annex to people like artists, poets and writers for months at a time, so they can do their work—painting and writing and meditating and thinking—in peace and quiet. It's what's called a "retreat". They're very sensitive, brainy and private people, completely immersed in their work. They love living like hermits. So don't disturb them, okay?'

I rolled my eyes. 'Aunty, but Lambu will not rest until she winkles out everything about them. You know how nosy she is!'

Chick kicked my shins hard under the table and glared at me. 'Bozo!' she warned, 'Watch your mouth.'

I grinned.

But I was right. Chick began spending a lot of time in the tree house, spying on the Annex. And gradually we began seeing more of our elusive 'ghosts' than ever before—they'd come out briefly into the verandahs, and even walked about in the overgrown garden. Strangely, their faces and limbs were always covered and they usually wore kurtas or kaftans. Oddly, if they spotted us, they quickly turned around and went back indoors. But there was no doubt—they were real people, not ghosts.

'You really shouldn't be such a nosy parker,' I told Chick one afternoon in the tree house as she riveted her binoculars on the two people who had just walked around the garden.

'Bozo, you don't know the half of it, so shut up!' she said turning to me. Her eyes were all gooey and shimmery. 'Don't you see? Even Mridula Aunty was trying to pull a fast one! They're not artists or writers or poets... Look at them!'

'So what are they? Aliens?'

'Honeymooners, you moron! Look how they're holding hands!'

'You've been reading too many of those trashy love-stories and they're getting to you,' I snorted. This was true—of late, Chick had been wasting a huge amount of time buried in stupid books with pink or mauve or yellow covers.

'Bah, what do you know? But this is so romantic!'

'Bah! Get a life!'

'Bozo!' I dodged as a cushion came flying my way. She turned her attention to the Annex again. 'How sweet of Mridula Aunty—and what a dead cool place to spend a honeymoon in!'

'Yeah,' I grinned, 'like you would know... How many have you had?'

I fled before she could catch me.

Well, we have something like fifty acres of unkempt garden, groves of trees and woodland, fields and wilderness in our domain to run wild in. Mridula Aunty is not exactly a tidy gardener and likes to let 'nature live its own life by its own rules'. She only interferes if, say, creepers start winding around the legs of our beds or we find a family of centipedes in the bathtub. We've been warned about, and trained to deal, with snakes, scorpions, centipedes and other creepy crawlies. Shaking out our clothes and shoes before wearing them has become second nature to us—especially during the monsoon when a lot of these guys want to share our private space. The training has paid off—no casualties till date, though there were several scares.

In addition, there's the beach and the sea, which here is quite safe (and calm) to swim in. (Except when invaded by the Portuguese Man-o-war jellyfish, which look like ink stains splotched on the sand.) This is because there's a massive wall-like rocky reef about half a mile out, on which all the big breakers first smash themselves to smithereens. Then they weakly slosh over the rocks and pour into the bay-cum-lagoon. At the southern end of the reef wall is a channel leading into the bay, and we've been forbidden from going anywhere close to this (marked with orange buoys) because of the currents that develop as the tides come in and out. At the southern end of the beach is a small stone jetty jutting into the sea, and a wooden boathouse where Dr D's pride and joy, his navy-blue and white 24-foot boat—The Lily of the West—is moored. It has sails as well as a pair of powerful outboard engines, a proper cabin with a couple of narrow bunks, a galley and bathroom. He calls it his yacht. Of course, we've been out in it many times, and often, he and Mridula Aunty use it to go to Mumbai, which takes about an hour and is much less effort than driving. They dock it at the Gateway and take a cab to wherever they want to go in town. Our parents call Dr D a 'shaukeen aadmi'—an enthusiast.

And get this! One year, our 'shaukeen' landlord and his pretty wife called us down to the jetty early one morning—all four of us. We had spent another night at their place because our parents were absentees as usual.

'Hurry up kids, come on now!' he boomed cheerfully as we followed sleepily.

'What is it, Uncle?' Chick groaned, 'It's so early!'

'You'll see!'

We gathered in a grumpy group on the jetty. At the end of it was a long log-like thing covered with a blue tarpaulin.

'This, my sweet lady and gentlemen, is your combined birthday presents for the year!' Dr D said as Mridula Aunty smiled. He turned to Lambu.

'If you will have the pleasure to unveil it, my dear...'

Chick walked over and slowly stripped the cover.

All of us gasped.

A resplendent turquoise and kingfisher-blue long wooden canoe lay beneath, with spangly silver and white waves painted along its sides, rather like Chick's swimsuit. At the stern, it had a sparkling white outboard engine.

'Wow!'

'She's yours. You have to christen her. I will teach you how to paddle and steer and use the engine, and how to maintain it.'

'Th...this is for us?' Chick stammered.

'Yes, and with great gifts comes great responsibility. There are two rules which go with her possession. If you break them, I will take her back. One: You will at no time leave the lagoon and take her out to open sea, without an experienced adult with you. That means, either I or Aunty or anyone we approve of. Two: You shall at all times wear life jackets—also supplied—when you take her out. Agreed?'

We grouped together.

'Better agree or he'll take it back!' Aslam said, greedily eyeing the canoe.

'We have to negotiate this,' Chick said. I tended to agree.

'Yeah, that life jacket part...' She nodded and turned to Dr D with a smile.

'Uncle, do we have to wear the life jackets all the time? You know how well we all swim—you and aunty taught us after all! It's so hot in summer... Besides, when we go swimming from the beach, we don't wear them.'

The man saw the point. He checked that Mridula Aunty agreed, and then nodded. 'All right, you three may be exempt, but not Sohail. He's still too small. But you three are responsible for him!' He glared at us. 'You have no idea what a time aunty and I had trying to convince your parents to let us give you this!'

'Thanks Dr D!'

'So, what are you going to call her?'

'We'll call her The Bedlam Boat!' Chick said, without batting an eyelid, let alone consulting me. But it was a good name, so I let it pass, and nodded briefly.

'Yeah, I was thinking the same thing.'

Beyond the rocky cliffs at the southern end of the beach is a small fishing village and beyond that is a bridge over a wide silver creek which leads to the small town (famous for its 'international' schools, one of which we attend), and then is the expressway to Mumbai. The steep rocky cliffs beyond the northern end of the beach go on for miles, with several almost inaccessible (from the land) small beaches and rocky coves and islets strewn along the way. Beyond the tip of the 'pincer-end' of the rocks forming the bay, at the northern end (we call them the 'Lobsters' Claws'), is a small rocky islet, separated from the rocky mainland by a 30-

foot channel of sea. Built on it, and towering up 150-foot, is a massive ancient turret-cum-tower, with narrow gun-slit windows in its round walls, along with a proper crenellated crown. Chick thinks it must have been an ancient lighthouse; I think it was probably a lookout post with a cannon mounted on top. The trouble is that try as we had, we hadn't been able to access it. First, we had to cross a small creek that flowed into the sea from the beach cliff, whose depth depended on whether the tide was in or out. Then we had to tackle a fearsome, lava field of scalpel sharp and treacherously slippery rocks, armed with shark-teeth barnacles that led upwards towards the pincer tip. It was riven by deep gullies and 'cheese-grater' slopes, interspersed with deep rock pools.

On one memorable weekend we made it to the pincer tip, looking as if we had taken part in a slasher movie. We looked across, at the tower looming gauntly above, and then down below at the sea swirling and swishing some 40 or 50 feet below us, washing over the rocks.

'No way across unless we somehow get down and swim,' I said, shaking my head. 'Besides, I can't see any doorway or entry point into the tower.'

Suddenly, she grabbed my arm and pointed. 'Bozo, look there...near those rocks... There's that dark hole—like a tunnel opening. Watch now, when the waves retreat you can see steps being exposed...steps leading upwards into the dark. It must be a tunnel and probably leads into the tower.'

I focused my bins on the spot. Chick was right. But we still had a problem.

'Yes, but we still have to get across to reach it!'

'You know, if we throw a rope across with a grappling hook, into that window there, we can establish a line across and we could cross using our hands and feet. Like the way pirates used to board sailing ships in the old days. And that window up there is big enough for us to squeeze through and get inside. We won't need the tunnel business.'

'And if we fall we'd either be smashed into pieces or be swept out to sea,' I said sardonically, 'so you try it and I'll follow!'

She glared at me. 'Very funny! You're the big Man Vs Wild Bear Grylls sucker, not me. So show me what you got!'

I was a big fan and we had had many arguments over the guy.

'He's the greatest,' I declared, 'he and that Mike fellow, with his chick!'

'What's so great about what they do? They've been trained in the Special Forces to do exactly that. Would you call a dog which has been trained to sit "great" when it sat when told to? They're military-trained survival experts, so they are just doing their job. Big deal! They're just showing off!'

'Hah…and I bet you have a huge crush on them!' I grinned and dodged as she lunged for me.

'It would be different if some paunchy slob like you managed to do a 100-foot chimney-sweep climb or whatever it's called.'

'If you can't tell the difference between six-pack abs and a paunch, you're going to have a tough time, babe!'

'Don't "babe" me, Bozo!'

Well, that time we had to return defeated. Chick had a set look on her face. 'There has got to be a way,' she said stubbornly and I knew she wouldn't give up. I was right. Our summer holidays started and none of us were going anywhere—parents had to work as usual, blah blah. Aslam was going for a short stay at a hill station right at the beginning of the holidays and thereafter was going to be busy preparing for a big music exam. His mom was quite the tiger mom, so he would be pretty much grounded till it was done. There was a glint in Chick's eyes as we joyfully got off the school bus on the last day before the holidays started.

'See,' she said belligerently, 'during these holidays, we will find a way across that channel and to the turret! That's our mission! And we start tomorrow! I've got a thick long rope.'

'What about a grappling iron thingy?'

She shook her head impatiently. 'We can try that too. If it doesn't work, we'll tie big knots along the rope and just throw it over the edge and climb down. It should be long enough. Then we will swim across to the tunnel entrance. Simple!'

'Pity Aslam's not here,' I said. She shrugged.

'Too bad! See you tomorrow morning at five,' Chick said. 'Tell no one! We have to do this in a hush-hush way. SOP (Standard Operation Procedure) applies!'

I nodded. 'Yeah. I'll have to sneak out without waking Sohail. He'll just follow us otherwise, whining and wailing all the way.'

'Can you imagine?' Chick said, her eyes shining. 'If we succeed we'd probably be the first people to explore the tower in hundreds of years! It may be littered with grinning skulls!'

'And heaps of gold coins and jewels too!'

'We might come back rich!'

'Hah!' I snorted, 'Alive would be nice!'

2

At 0500 hours the next morning, we two shinned down the stout drainpipes and thick madhumalti creepers growing outside our respective verandahs (SOP) and rendezvoused in the garden below. The Dubashes were early risers too; Mridula Aunty had to get ready for her first dog training session at 7 a.m. and Dr D jogged on the beach, so we had to make tracks before they came out. Our own parents got up at around 7.30 a.m.

Chick had her faithful black backpack and was clad in thick blue jeans and a denim full-sleeved shirt. They would provide some protection against those jagged sharp rocks. I was also in thick khaki full-length cargoes and a button-down safari shirt.

I nodded approvingly. 'Good! Better sweaty than slashed to ribbons,' I remarked laconically and she raised her eyebrows.

We both had tough hiking boots—another measure to protect ourselves from those serrated shark-teeth Black Diamond rocks. She looked at my backpack.

'Got everything?'

'Affirmative! Swiss knife, Maglite, energy bars, water canteen, phone, lighter, first-aid...' I had the works. I had seen where we were going. Be prepared. Be vigilant. That's me. Besides, it was SOP.

'You got what you need?' I asked.

'The rope and some other stuff,' she said. Her eyes narrowed. 'Swimming trunks on underneath?'

'We're under SOP, remember!' I said. 'And you?'

'In the backpack.'

We always carried our swimming things along on such expeditions. You never knew when they'd come handy—or when you'd simply want to cool off in the sea after a tough hot trek or climb. Besides, the Black Diamond Rocks' 'lava field' had several deep, clear rocky pools.

'Now come on, Bozo, let's go!' Her dark eyes glinted like a leopard that had just spotted a fawn. We climbed over the gate at the garden-end (it had a deadbolt that squealed like a stuck piglet) and went down the rocky steps to the beach.

'We'll keep to the cliffs' shadow,' Chick said, striding ahead, 'but watch out for the spinifex.' I usually let Chick lead on such expeditions, she loves it when she thinks she is the boss (otherwise she can be a pain). It is just like when the commander of an aircraft lets the first officer fly the plane, but is always ready to take control if necessary. Besides I have to watch her back—girls sometimes do the daftest things.

The sky was still dark blue, with high fleecy clouds just beginning to turn pink and gold and orange in the east—pretty, I suppose. The tide was out, the sea sighing softly. There was not a soul around. We headed north towards the Black Diamond lava field. The creek was 15–20 feet wide; it came out of the cliffs and joined the sea and could get shoulder-deep and pretty tricky when the tide came in. We were forbidden from crossing it until we reached our teens, and even then, we were strongly advised not to cross over during high tide. But we had crossed it many times subsequently, and had perfected the technique: Avoid high tide, hold hands firmly and wade across, each one ready to pull the other up in case he or she lost balance or stepped into a trough. We hadn't explored the Black Diamond lava field properly, because the rocks invariably cut us up. Now we removed our boots and socks and rolled up our jeans as high as we could and waded across, hand in hand. This morning, because the tide was out, it was just over knee-deep—no problem. Then, firmly booted up again, we tackled the jagged rocks of the lava field.

It was easier this time around, with our tough clothes and boots protecting us somewhat from nicks and grazes. The rocks were arranged in a series of serried steps, interspersed with gullies glinting with rock pools, and narrowing as they reached the pincer tip. It was hard climbing, especially since the rocks were serrated and slimy and sometimes brittle. Both of us were sweaty by the time we scrambled over the last set of 'steps' to the pincer's edge. We squatted on our haunches and looked at each other. This was it. Chick took out the rope from her backpack. It was thick and long as a python and must have been quite heavy to lug around. She'd already made the knots, so it was ready. Then she grinned wickedly and delved into her bag again. Something metallic clunked and she drew out a grappling boat hook with multiple prongs.

'I borrowed this from the boathouse yesterday evening,' she said. 'Let's tie the rope to this and throw it across into one of those window openings.'

We chucked the grappling hook across, with the rope attached to it, taking turns. Sometimes the damn thing fell short, other times, it just skidded off the side of the tower, or bounced off the window ledge we were aiming at.

'Damn!' Chick said, 'Now duck, I'm going to swing this round my head like a lasso and let it fly!'

It soared across the chasm, landed with a solid 'thwunk'—and lodged firmly inside the window. I rolled my eyes.

'You got lucky, kid!'

'Got it!' she said exultantly. Of course I could have done

it too, but was glad she had managed to. Good for the team morale, you see.

'Let's test it,' she said and we both gripped the rope and tugged. It seemed quite firmly lodged in the window at the other end.

'Looks good,' she grunted as we gave it another mighty heave, 'it'll take our weight!' Just then, with a clatter the grappling iron broke free and two big loose rocks that formed the window ledge, crashed down into the sea, leaving the window gaping larger than before. We somersaulted backwards on top of each other like a pile of tossed laundry.

'Oof!'

'Mmmph!'

For a moment, Chick clung to me in sheer panic, I think, and then, we quickly disentangled ourselves and stood up. Like I say, a chick needs a guy to hang onto in moments of crisis. Her face was red.

'Well, that's too risky,' she said, stating the obvious and smoothing down her shirt while shaking her head. 'And your ears have gone all red.'

'Funny how Bear Grylls has no problem at all,' I remarked. 'Just tosses the rope across a couple of times and that's it—he's over like a gibbon! Wonder how he does it.'

'Hah! I'll bet there are guys at the other end making sure his rope is firmly anchored,' she said, and for the first time, I began wondering if that might indeed be true.

'Okay, we'll have to do this the other way. We need to tie one end around a really solid rock,' Chick said, looking around.

'Make sure the rock is not serrated, or it'll just cut through the rope.'

We found a pillar-like extension of the pincer rock itself—no chance of anything coming loose here—and tied the rope around it. Then, both of us tested it, pulling back with all our strength.

'That's good!' she said, dusting her hands, her face red with exertion. She took the free end of the rope and lowered it over the pincer's edge. We peered over. Good, it was long enough—we could see it rest on the rocks at the bottom.

'I'll go first,' I said. It was time for the commander to take over. She might think she was one tough cookie but she was still a girl.

'No way, Bozo,' she said, her eyes flashing. 'It was my idea, so it has to be my neck!' Briskly, she tied up her hair into a high topknot. I shrugged. I guess sometimes you have to let your co-pilot fly solo. How else would they learn? This was one of those times.

'You trying to be Modesty Blaise?' I grinned.

'Better than her, Wee Willie!'

'Just watch out, will you?'

She nodded as she got down and gripped the rope, wriggling carefully to the edge. I watched like a hawk, ready for action. Holding on for dear life, she backed over the edge and suddenly, with a grunt and scream of surprise, she was swinging free, in mid-air, right over the channel. The rope creaked and strained as it took her weight. I peered over the overhang's bulge. She was swinging from side to side, looking down and then up at me.

'Are you okay?' I bellowed. 'Or should I pull you up?'

'I'm fine!' she nodded, her face red, clutching on to one of the thick knots in the rope. Then, with her ankles crossed around the rope for grip, she began lowering herself bit by bit. At last she was down, standing on the rocks below and looking up and grinning triumphantly.

'Come on, Bozo, what're you waiting for?'

Cautiously, with my backpack still slung on, I got down to my knees, gripped the rope and very slowly began lowering myself.

My stomach registered a whole squadron of butterflies taking off as I suddenly swung free over empty air, and braced my feet so I wouldn't smash into the rocky cliff-side. I lowered myself, my arms taking the strain and my ankles gripping the rough rope tightly. Then, Chick was reaching out to me and caught me around the waist as I slithered down the last few feet.

'Gotcha, Bozo!' she grinned, 'Isn't this cool?'

But boy, I could have sworn she had hugged me briefly there.

Perched on the rocks, we looked around. To our left—or the south—was a wall of rocks, largely blocking the sea's exit. It swished in from our right (the north) and swirled around and against and over the rock wall. Ahead and just below us was the channel, maybe 25 to 30 feet across; at the moment appearing quite shallow because we could see the 'mouth' of the tunnel just across, with only the bottom half under water. Chick pointed and grinned.

'No problem! We can do it! And the water doesn't seem very deep, and it's just a few feet across.'

'Good!' She looked around. 'You sit here and turn around and face that way. I'm going behind those rocks to change!' she said, taking her backpack and going behind a jumble of low rocks near the cliff face. They really were too low for her to hide behind adequately, but Chick doesn't fuss too much about such things, and trusts me, which is something I appreciate about her—when a job's gotta be done, it's gotta be done, period. I duly turned around and faced the channel. She emerged in minutes, in her electric-and-sky blue counter-shaded swimsuit, (which made her look like she was wearing sunlit waves) and stuffed her clothes into her backpack. Its snazzy colours and deep neckline made her look real cool—sleek and sinuous as a shark spearing through the water, though catch me telling her that. I stripped to my trunks.

'Let's go! We'll leave our clothes here.'

'I'll take my backpack. It's waterproof and has all our vital stuff.'

We sat at the edge of the rocks, side by side, and then slid off it, like we were getting into a swimming pool. Well, it was deeper than I'd expected, the water slopped over our shoulders. We trod water, looked at each other, and turned and swam towards the other side, where the tunnel mouth was. Only the top quarter part of it was exposed now; the tide was turning.

'Come on, Bozo! Let's check it out,' she said, as we swam up to the dark tunnel mouth. Her voice was breathless with excitement.

'Hope the steps keep going up and not down. It won't be fun to be trapped in a flooded tunnel!'

'Just come on!' We held our breath and ducked our heads just under the water at the entrance, just so we wouldn't bump them on the tunnel roof inches above. The water swilled about over our chins as we bent at the tunnel entrance. I gripped her hand to reassure her. Side by side and bumping into each other gently, we suddenly stubbed our toes at exactly the same moment. We clutched each other for balance.

'Ouch!'

'Hey Bozo, be careful of the steps. They're going up!'

They were and as we climbed them, the water receded again, and streamed off us. Chick took out my Maglite and flashed it ahead. The tunnel ran straight ahead upwards. The walls were made of cut rock.

'What's that clattering noise?' I asked, cocking my head.

'Must be crabs slithering over the rocks.' She flashed the torch around. 'Look, there's one. God, he's humongous!'

The steps, shallow at first, became steeper as we approached the other end, and the tunnel finally ended at what seemed to be the bottom of a well-shaft.

'Bozo, don't you see? We're now inside the tower at the bottom!' Chick whispered. She was thrilled, and flashed the torch along the walls. They rose above us. Small narrow gun-slits and the occasional wider window let columns of musty blue daylight in. Rocky steps built into the wall spiralled around the walls of the tower. They led up to a gallery—without a safety railing—running right around it at the top. A doorway in the gallery wall probably led to the lookout post. The bottom of the shaft comprised a pool of glinting black and silver water, glimmering dark green and blue where the sunbeams hit it, surrounded by a jumble of rocks, going around the base, and on what we stood.

'We've done it at last! Now let's go up!' Chick was as excited as a kid in Disneyland. She looked at the pool, 'That looks inviting too, but let's go up first! We'll check it out when we return.'

We ascended the rocky steps carefully, me leading again. 'Gimme your hand,' I said, reaching out. She gave me a quirky look but her hand too. I was taking no chances. We kept as close to the wall as we could because there was no railing. The rocky steps seemed firmly embedded into the walls, and we only had to be careful we didn't slip on any moss or slime. They just seemed to go on and on and were dizzyingly round.

'This is like something out of *The Lord of the Rings*,' Chick suddenly whispered, her lips brushing my ear and making me jump. She softly bumped into me from behind.

At the top, there was a wide gallery running around the inside circumference, and a doorway leading out onto the 'terrace' of the tower.

We emerged at last, panting into daylight, blinking in the sun.

'Bozo, we've done it! On our very first attempt! I can't believe it! Gimme five, man! Wow. We must be the first human beings here in five-hundred years!'

'Yeah, probably, but you gotta be cool.' I narrowed my eyes and looked around, watchful for snakes.

'Just look at the view. Hey, did you bring your binoculars?'

The view was stunning, got to say that. We were high above the long curving golden beach. Even Bedlam House, glimmering in the sun in the distance on the plateau amongst the trees, was lower down. To the west, the sea shimmered in various shades of blue-grey, blue-green and deep blue, spangled with sunlight and pinpricked with black fishing boats, far out. What had the lookouts here been watching out for? Strange sailing ships approaching menacingly, flying hostile, unknown colours?

A stone plinth ran around the inside of the wall, which made a convenient bench to sit on. We sat side by side and I nodded slowly.

'You did good!' I said. Her eyes flashed and I quickly added, 'We both did good!' Boy, was she touchy or what!

We were both hot and sticky, though there was a stiff breeze coming off the sea that cooled us quickly.

'I'm doing a recce,' I said, getting to my feet. I prowled around, between the rocks, peering into cracks and crannies, looking around for a cannon. But there was no sign of any, big or small.

The circumference of the tower must have been 50 or 60 feet. Right opposite the entrance, jutting directly over the sea, was a small stone cubicle or room, sheltered from the elements by its stone roof. It was probably where the guard on lookout duty took shelter when it rained or when there was a storm; a sort of guardhouse. He could keep an eye on the sea and remain dry (and unseen) at the same time.

'Watch out for snakes and scorpions,' Chick warned, opening my backpack and taking out the canteen and energy bars.

'Ya, ya, I know!'

I picked up a stick and started prodding at some foliage and dry grass that had somehow managed to grow out of one side of the wall and had tumbled onto the floor. There were a lot of creepy crawlies that scattered and scuttled as I probed, and I soon stopped. I ducked and entered the little guardhouse. It was dim after the bright sunlight outside and it took my eyes several seconds to adjust. It was also cooler. Half the room was almost buried in the silvery scrunchy sand, made up of finely crushed shells. It had piled high against the inside wall like a huge snowdrift against a house, blown in by the sea through the lookout slits over god knows how many centuries. I sat down, leaning my head back against the pile. It was cool and comfortable. I poked my head out and called Chick.

'Hey, stop baking out there and come inside! It's real cool here.'

She came in and sat down beside me, leaning her head back against the sandy cushion.

'Mission accomplished!' I said. 'Now, what do we do for the rest of the summer?'

'This is so cool!' She took a gulp of water and then a bite of an energy bar. 'I'm going to have a snooze,' she murmured unexpectedly, yawning, 'we got up damn early for this expedition!' She wriggled a bit, leaning back against the sand heap and made herself comfortable and shut her eyes. Like I said, chicks do the daftest things. Catch me napping under such circumstances! Besides, someone had to keep watch.

'Okay, you have a nap,' I said kindly, 'you must be fagged out. I'll keep watch for scorpions.' She opened one eye and glared at me.

'Bozo!' she warned.

I went and stood at the gun-slit window and looked out at the sea, wondering who had done this last. He must have seen pretty much the same thing. Then I looked straight down. I expected to see waves dashing at the base of the tower, but they weren't. The water was calm, like it was in the lagoon, heaving slightly but not frothy mad or anything. I focused on the reef and gulped. At its northern end, the reef, instead of running parallel to the beach, extended out into the sea, and roughly followed the contours of the pincer tip and islet, before straightening out and running parallel to the coast again for a bit. But the reef seemed to end a little way beyond this because I could see the creamers rushing in on to the beaches on the far northern side.

'This sand is real cool,' Chick murmured contentedly. I looked at her; she'd literally buried herself up to the neck in it and was grinning at me. She looked weird with that topknot sticking out from the top of her head like a French roll.

'You look like an extra in Beau Geste. Don't complain when you get sand or crabs inside your swimsuit,' I said, 'you're asking for it.'

'The sand will wash away when we swim.'

'Uh-huh.' I turned back to the view.

'Urgghmph... Something's poking my back!' Chick muttered a little later, squirming. I turned around again. She had gotten up and was on her knees, scooping out the heap of sand piled high against the wall like a dog digging for a bone.

'Umph... There's something buried here...'

She scooped out a fistful of sand, and something whitish glimmered briefly before the sand cascaded down over it again.

'Bozo, what was that?' she asked, her voice rising.

'Dunno...didn't see it properly. Dig it out—must be a shell or something.'

I got down beside her and we began digging.

'Bloody hell!' I said, hoarsely backing away. 'Oh shit!'

'Th…that's a p…p…pelvic bone jutting out…' Chick stuttered. 'I'm sure of it; I have just done it in Biology!'

'Th…there must be a skeleton there…' I whistled long and low. 'As they say, be careful what you wish for!'

'I…I did not…'

We looked at each other.

'Should we dig more?' I asked, wondering if she was going to scream or faint or go running down the steps. My own heart was galloping like a racehorse. 'You won't be sick or faint or something?'

She gave me the look again.

'We have to! I couldn't live with myself otherwise,' she said flatly.

'Come on then!'

'What if it rises from the dead or something?' she asked suddenly.

'Then we're screwed! Still want to go on or should we go back?'

She nodded. 'We dig,' she said briefly.

Got to hand it to her—Chick had guts.

Hot and sweaty, and with hammering hearts, we regarded the fruits of our labour some ten minutes later. In the dim light of the little guardhouse, two small skeletons glimmered. They didn't grin up at us in the usual macabre way you see in movies. You see, the skulls and skeletons were facing each other, close up, almost teeth against teeth. Their arms and legs were completely entangled around each other, their foreheads joined like Siamese twins.

'Oh my god!' Chick whispered, clutching my hand. 'Look at them! They died in each others' arms. It looks like they were kissing! They must have been lovers! Like Romeo and Juliet. How tragic!'

Like I said, she was into all that mushy stuff.

'Or they were trying to kill each other and succeeded,' I said succinctly. 'I've seen mynas and sparrows fighting exactly like this—face-to-face on the ground, claws enmeshed, eyes glaring, murder in their hearts, ready to kill!'

She glared at me.

'But they're so small! They must have been kids or something.'

'What do we do now? Report this to the cops?'

'Why?' Chick demanded, her eyes flashing. 'Those two are long dead and gone, poor things, so let them rest in peace here. Why should we disturb them?'

'Because they must belong to someone. They must have families! Someone might still be looking for them.'

'Huh?' she snorted. 'I don't think they had families that cared very much about them if this is how they ended up, poor things! Look, we've managed to get to this place at last. If we tell anyone what we've found, there'll be hordes of people stomping all over and they'll be asking us why we came here in the first place and all sorts of nosy questions. The press will be blundering around like a herd of buffaloes. It'll be turned into a mela. They'll probably forbid us from coming here again. Besides, it's not wise to disturb the dead!'

That way, Chick was right.

'Let's see if there's anything else we can find,' she said and bravely stepped towards the bones. I nodded and joined her.

'Their clothes must have rotted and blown away,' she said, frowning. 'God knows how long they've been lying here. The sand has preserved them perfectly.'

'Can you tell if they're girls or boys?' I asked, diffidently.

Chick nodded. 'There's something about the pelvis...' she murmured and leant over and whispered exactly what in my ear. I went scarlet.

'But I don't want to touch them or examine them.' She looked at me, 'They must have been girl and boy or…well, whatever they were, they liked each other enough to end up like this.'

'I guess. So, what now?'

'I think we should just cover them up again and leave them in peace. But let us dig around a bit to see if there's anything else we can find before we do that.'

We dug around a bit, but found nothing.

Then, my phone rang.

'Oh, crap…it's HQ… Hello, ya, hi Ma…Yeah I'm with Lambu, we went for a walk… Sohail was sleeping and you said not to wake him… Okay, we're coming back!'

Chick grinned at me. 'RPG (rocket propelled grenade) from HQ?' she asked sympathetically.

'Yeah. Sohail awoke and found me gone and threw a tantrum!'

'We'd better go back. She looked at the half-exposed skeletons. 'Let's bury Romeo and Juliet properly again.'

We went down and looked at the glimmering pool at the bottom.

'We'll check this out another time. Come on, let's go,' Chick said.

And boy, Houston, did we have a problem. The tide had come in, and a section of the tunnel was flooded to the roof. We'd have to swim underwater, maybe the length of half a swimming pool, through the tunnel to emerge at its mouth at the other end. Or else, we could wait for the tide to turn—and everyone at Bedlam House to submerge into hysterics.

'Swim or wait?' I asked as we stared at the frothy wavelets swishing eagerly over our feet.

'Swim. It's not too far.'

'Okay, I'll go first. Thank god the Maglite's waterproof.'

'Yeah!'

I waded in and she followed.

It was tougher than we had expected, because the water kept pushing us backwards as the tide was still coming in. We focused on the glimmer of light at the end of the tunnel and swam as hard as we could towards it, holding our breaths. We popped out like champagne corks, our breath whooshing, and then grabbed each other as the waves sloshed around and buffeted us.

'Hang on, it's turbulent!' I spluttered. A wave swooped in like a predator, whooshed around the rocky cul-de-sac, and like a giant rinsing out his mouth, buffeted me hard in the back, sweeping me face down towards the main channel and the open sea beyond.

Chick screamed and turned. One long brown arm shot out and grabbed my trunks and yanked back hard as I sort of body surfed past her. The wave swished under me and I bobbed up and down, vertical again, treading water and spluttering as water slopped into my mouth. Something clammy was tangling and clinging to my ankles and I kicked hard. It could have been a bloody octopus trying to take me down, man. And to my horror, I saw my trunks float up and away as another wave circled in for the snatch. Chick gave a scream of laughter and I saw her streak towards them.

'Yours, I believe,' she said, returning moments later, controlling her giggles with difficulty—she was holding my trunks up. 'Here. Come on, Bozo, we better get out of the water; it's pretty rough here.'

She was right. But man, no way was I going to get out without my trunks on. I staggered towards the edge and when tummy-deep, I tried slipping them on. I was promptly knocked ass over head by another wave and floundered, flat on my back.

'Oh crap!'

Chick hauled herself out, turned around, looked at me and

raised a sardonic eyebrow, grinning from ear to ear. 'If you've finished doing your cabaret number, you can come out and put them on, you moron. I won't rescue you again if you get swept away.' She turned towards the rope dangling down. 'I'm going up! No point changing now. We have to cross the creek and the water will be much higher now. We'll get wet again. Let's wear our shoes though.'

Scarlet-faced, I clambered out and dragged on my trunks, tying the cord firmly.

'That's not SOP!' I told her.

'Forget it for a bit, will you? You know, I hate wearing clothes over a wet, sandy swimsuit.'

I shrugged. 'Okay, then.'

Big mistake: Never mess with SOP or nature.

We got to the top, hauled up our rope and coiled it away. Got to admit—it was nice feeling the sea breeze cool our sweaty bare bodies as we clambered over and through the lava field gullies. We reached one of the steep rocky inclines which was maybe twelve-feet high and had to be manoeuvred on hands and feet. At its base was one of the deep still rocky pools that we skirted around. Chick, with her gibbon's limbs, went up first. I began to follow but found myself slithering down every time. At the top, she turned around, sat down and leaned forward, extending a hand.

'Here!' she grunted, 'Grab my hand!'

Sometimes you gotta make your co-pilot feel indispensable. Like I said, it's good for morale. I looked up at her and took her hand.

'Gotcha Bozo!' she grunted, 'And don't try to look down the top of my swimsuit.'

'I'm 15, so what do you expect?' I got another murderous glare.

'Ready?' She heaved. I took a mighty step up as she yanked,

and then, she lost her seating. With a scream, she came sliding down on her back, letting go of my hand, rather like a kid coming down a slide. I slithered back down, desperately clutching at the rock face. I came to a halt on my knees at the bottom and looked up just as she crashed into me, her arms locking around my back for support. For a moment, we teetered in a tight clinch, eyeballing each other, and then tumbled into the rock pool behind us with a mighty splash. Underwater, our legs and arms got briefly entangled and entwined, and then very quickly, we drew apart.

'Ouch, ow! Oh shit!'

'Ouch, ouch! Oh damn!'

We waded out, red as hell and wincing. Chick grimaced, twisted around and looked at her back.

'You okay?' I snapped, trying to conceal my discomfiture. She didn't look very okay.

'Turn around!'

Meekly, she did. God almighty! Her back, right from her neck and shoulder, down to her waist, the back of her arms and thighs—they were all nastily grazed; lined and woven with long cuts and scratches now welling blood that had begun to trickle down. Likewise, my palms, forearms and knees were also netted with cuts. The Black Diamond rocks had made us both pay in blood.

'You okay? Shit, there's blood running down your back!' I said, appalled by the state of her back. She twisted her head around some more.

'Dab them with Betadine,' she said, wincing. 'But first, we have to get up. I don't want to tumble down a second time.'

'Like Jack and Jill,' I said, sotto voce.

'Don't be corny!'

We managed to get up the second time round without a hitch.

I took out the Betadine ointment and started dabbing her cuts with gentle pats of my bare fingers—from her neck and working down to the small of her back.

She squirmed. 'It's cool and feels nice!'

'There's no way to bandage all this,' I said, frowning. 'The nicks are all over the place. I'm doing the back of your thighs now, okay?'

'Roger.' She stood still as I lightly applied the ointment.' Do they hurt?'

'I'll live. Thanks, Bozo!'

'Welcome!'

She stared at me. 'Hey, you're cut up too! Show me your arms—my turn now.'

I could have done it myself of course, but I let her. Chicks like nursing and bandaging and stuff like that.

'There!' she said, 'That should do for now!'

Then, bloody but unbowed, we reached the creek. The water was now almost chest-deep and muscled us around strongly, pushing us leeward. We held each other's hands tightly and crossed carefully. The cuts stung sharply in the salt water. The Betadine got washed away.

'Your trunks fastened firmly?' she asked, before we entered. I glowered back at her.

'Very funny!'

'It was,' she snorted as I retied them just to be sure. You can make a mistake once, but twice is unforgivable.

'Seriously,' I said, changing the subject. 'What we found this morning, awesome, wasn't it?'

'Yes. And we have to keep it a secret.'

'What about Aslam? Do we tell him?'

She made a face. 'Oh, he'll want to go and see the skeletons for himself and maybe hang them in his room or something. You know how he likes to collect weird stuff.'

'He'll be mad if he comes to know… Besides, he's my wingman.' Up went the eyebrows again.

'Let's play it by ear. Besides, it's pretty dangerous getting there.'

I rolled my eyes and glanced at our war wounds. 'Tell me about it, Chick! Have to say, you did pretty well.' I nodded approvingly, back in command. Give credit where it's due, that's my motto.

'Hmm…well, certainly better than you! At least my swimsuit didn't come off in a crisis!'

'Where did you go? Why did you leave me? I was awake and you left me! I'll tell Mama!' Sohail came charging out of Bedlam House as soon as he saw us enter the garden gate. In the lawn a motley bunch of dogs stood in a semicircle with their owners, around Mridula Aunty, who was putting them through their paces. Night, the Dubashes's lovely Rottweiler (and a complete dodo—he let Cushion bully him) sat beside her, his pink tongue hanging out, as if showing the others what a good dog he was. We scuttled around the garden, keeping a low profile so as to not disrupt the class. Actually, Mridula Aunty didn't mind—she said the dogs must learn to obey commands even under the most chaotic circumstances and surroundings.

'You went swimming and never took me!' Sohail whined as we went up the steps into the lobby.

There was a gleam in Chick's eyes and she suddenly lunged for Sohail and pinched his plump cheeks. He has curly hair and chubby cheeks and most girls over thirteen can't resist him.

'Bhaiyya tell her, she's pinching me!' Sohail wailed.

Chick bent down and kissed him. Sohail broke free and fled

up the stairs, frantically rubbing his cheeks.

'He's too cute,' she gushed, 'I just love his cheeks; like rosogullas. I could eat him!'

'You're welcome to. Try living with him!' I said sourly.

A small dog, almost completely covered with silky dark golden curls, came charging down the steps, yapping shrilly. Often it was difficult to tell which end was which.

'Oh oh, here comes the Cactus!'

'Cushion! Come here, baby!' The dog scampered towards Chick and leapt into her arms. Then she wriggled around and started yapping shrilly, baring her sharp little teeth at me. Chick giggled.

'She thinks you've been up to no good with me! It's okay Cushy; he's been a gentleman, even if he did take his trunks off in front of me!' I went purple.

'I did no such thing, you...you...!' I sputtered to a halt.

'Cool it Bozo, just kidding!'

'We meet at the tree house at 1100 hours to postmortem this morning,' I said briefly. She looked at me.

'Yes, it was awesome, wasn't it?'

The door to Dr D's clinic opened and a lady with a little girl in a pink dress emerged, the girl tugging at her mother's hand. Her head was bandaged but she kept looking at a small, shiny silver-and-maroon medal pinned to her dress. Dr D loomed behind them, peering over his reading glasses, smiling and waving. The two gold teeth in his mouth glinted.

'Bye Lavania, you were very brave! Braver than even a soldier!'

'Thank you doctor,' the lady said as they went down the steps. The little girl stopped and stared at the dogs on the lawn.

'Mama, look!' she pointed.

'Yes, that's a doggie school,' her mom said as their car drove up to the portico.

Dr D grinned at us. 'You two hellion lovebirds have been up to no good, I take it?' he boomed, winking at us. 'Ah, just back from a romantic dawn swim, by the looks of it!'

I went red and glared at him.

'What happened to her, Uncle?' Chick asked, completely unfazed.

'She was running and tripped and hit her head on the corner of a table!' He grinned. 'She was such a brave little thing I had to give her a medal!' He raised his shaggy brows. 'Your holidays have started?'

We nodded.

'Good! Be wicked, kids. Remember, you'll only be young once and don't forget to put on sunscreen when you're out on the beach!' He smiled genially and began singing 'The Young Ones' in his deep baritone; he obviously thought the lyrics pertained to us, ('....and the young ones, shouldn't be afraid... To live, love... when the flame is strong...') his eyes twinkling merrily. Suddenly, he stopped and his eyes narrowed as he saw the state we were in. His eyebrows shot up. We turned to flee up the stairs.

'You two!' he roared, 'Get back down here! What the hell happened to both of you?' He strode over. 'Slashed and bloody! You've been playing on those terrible rocks again, haven't you?'

'Dr D, we put Betadine ointment. We're fine!' Chick protested, squirming.

'We always take first-aid with us!'

'Get inside the cave right now!' he barked, with a beckoning forefinger. 'The Ogre will see you now!'

And give us tetanus shots, no doubt!

'We're fine, Uncle!'

'Inside! Both of you! On the double!'

He followed us in. 'Sophia, get a first-aid tray ready!' he yelled at his nurse. 'Spirit, tincture-iodine, fully-loaded 12-calibre Magnum syringe—the usual! I have two idiot kids who've been playing with rusty cheese graters!'

'Nitu baby, what have you been doing?' Sophia asked horrified as she eyed Chick's back. She'd been with Dr Dubash for donkeys' years and had seen us grow up.

Dr D sat down on his rotating stool, grinned like Shrek, and squinted down his spectacles at Chick's brown back, dipping a wad of cotton wool in antiseptic. He had gently begun cleaning her shoulder when his mobile rang. He frowned impatiently.

'Yes? Dr Dubash here...'

The frown got deeper. He nodded to Sophia, indicating she take over and then got off his stool and went to the window, cupping his hand over the phone.

'What? They are on the same train? Are you sure? Well, just lie low. Hanji, don't worry...this evening at 8 o'clock...*pakka*... everything will be fine! Everything is ready here! *Theek hain...* we'll be there at CST...it should be okay, it's very crowded, so easy not to be seen. Take care now.'

He disconnected and got back to Chick.

'Hmm...' he suddenly grunted, peering through his spectacles perched at the tip of his nose. He strapped on his head-mounted torch and switched it on.

'Umm...darling, will you lie down a moment, there's a shard of quartz winking at me from your back which I have to get out...'

Chick lay down on her tummy, looking a little apprehensive as Dr D took out a pair of tweezers from his sterilizer. 'Sweetheart, this might just be a little uncomfortable because I might have to probe a little...okay? Try not to squirm.'

'Okay, Uncle...'

Shit, Dr D was using his 'gentle' voice—which meant it was going to hurt. I went up to Chick and took her hand. You gotta be with your guys when the chips are down.

Poor chicklet—it did hurt because she squeezed her eyes shut and winced suddenly. She let out a little 'unhh!' and gripped my hand tightly. I dared not look at what Dr D was doing.

'There you go, sweetheart!' he said, depositing a glistening sliver of quartz on the kidney tray Sophia was holding, with a clink. 'I'll just dress this now...' He was done in two minutes. 'Good as new!'

Chick got up; there was a strange shimmer in her eyes as she looked at me.

'You okay, Bozo?' she asked, 'You've gone absolutely white!'

'Yeah, yeah, I'm fine!' I blustered, 'You're the one that has had bullets removed, remember...'

Dr D regarded us both with raised eyebrows and a sardonic smile.

'I'm giving you both tetanus shots,' he said, priming the syringe. 'This should cover you for this and all the scrapes you get into during the holidays. Those rocks are full of evil bacteria... If the nicks are inflamed or painful tomorrow, come and see me again.'

'Thanks Uncle,' we said meekly after he'd finished with us. He gave us a tube of ointment. 'Apply this after you bathe,' he said, 'it'll soothe the pain and reduce any inflammation.'

'Thanks, Uncle.'

'No medals for you two,' he grinned as he saw us out. (It was a custom with him to personally see his patients to the door). 'But I'll send you the bill!'

'Um...Uncle, please don't tell our moms about this,' Chick said, turning on her sweetest smile and putting on her shirt over her swimsuit. She made a face. 'You know what moms are like! They'll ground us.'

Dr Dubash winked, nodded slowly, and carefully shut the door.

We met as scheduled at 1100 hours in the tree house. Thankfully, Mom, had taken Sohail to the orthodontist in town—he would probably need braces—so we could talk freely. Whenever Sohail came up to the tree house, we had to be extra vigilant and keep an eye on him all the time. Thirty feet up in the canopy, surrounded by restless green leaves, it was cool in the tree house. I winced as I climbed up the rope ladder trying to protect my palms. Chick was already there, looking uncomfortable—something was bugging her. She was in a long grey skirt and a baggy orange and white T-shirt. She fidgeted and squirmed.

'Listen Bozo, do me a favour,' she said, taking out the tube of ointment Dr D had given us. 'I managed to put this on my legs but not my back and I can't ask Ma to do so… She'll freak. So will you? The damn back's burning!'

'Uh, okay, I don't mind!'

She turned her back towards me.

'Okay, lift my top up from the back right up to my shoulders,' she said.

Deadpan, I did, trying to keep the material from chafing against her back. She was right—some of the abrasions and weals looked red and angry. Gently, I began applying the ointment. Dr D had only dressed the cut from where he had removed the shard of quartz. I was getting used to this kind of thing. And weirdly, I liked the soft feel of her shoulder and back and skin under my fingers.

'Thanks,' she said after I had finished and very gently lowered her top back down. 'It felt really nice! You have a cool touch! I liked it!'

'No problem,' I shrugged. 'Anytime!'

We made ourselves comfortable with the cushions; she lying on her tummy, me propped up against a wall.

'So, we tell no one about what we found this morning?' I said, keen to get back on track and make matters clear.

Chick nodded. 'Yes. But I wonder how those two got there in the first place. I doubt they could have come the same way we had.'

I nodded, hooding my eyes. 'Good point. Maybe they came by boat...'

'That's possible. Maybe they were shipwrecked.'

Then I remembered. 'Lambu, there is a way! You know, before we found the skeletons, I was looking down from the tower? Here's the thing: You can get to the front of the base of the tower—the side facing the sea—without leaving our lagoon. The reef extends beyond that. Any boat can land there—either from our lagoon or from the open sea on the northern side. We got so excited by those skeletons that I just forgot! Then, all they have to do is to come around the base of the tower. There must be an entrance into the base of the tower which we missed. Once you're there, you simply climb up like we did.'

'Wow! You mean we did that hair-raising climb over the lava field for nothing?'

'Well it was exciting...'

'And painful,' she added, wincing. 'Really, I think I'm going to change back into my swimsuit—it leaves the back bare; this way the cloth chafes against it.'

'Tell you what! We'll go there again in The Bedlam.'

'Today?'

'Why not? We could take The Bedlam out in the afternoon. Say 1500 hours—everyone's snoring then!'

'Great!'

I glanced out of the tree house towards the Annex and stiffened. There had been a movement across the windows.

'Hey, someone's in the Annex,' I said, picking up my bins. Chick shifted and came next to me. She'd washed her hair with some fragrant shampoo.

'Let me see!'

The doors leading to the balcony of the first floor slid open.

'Oh,' I said, 'it's only Mridula Aunty.'

She took the glasses from me.

'She's dusting the place,' she said, sounding surprised. 'Oh, they're probably expecting tenants.'

I frowned, my antenna suddenly twitching. 'But why should she dust the place personally? They've got staff to do that sort of thing.'

Chick grinned wickedly. 'Tenants sometimes leave valuables or other kind of things which Mridula Aunty might not like the staff to find,' she said dryly. 'She's probably just checking.'

'Hmm...I guess.'

'So we meet this afternoon! SOP applies again!'

She nodded and grinned. 'Great! And this time, hopefully, we'll try and not get caught by the tide and won't have to slide down cheese-grater rock faces.'

So that's what we did. In the heat of the afternoon, we sneaked out again. Sohail was thankfully sleeping in Mom and Dad's bedroom—because they had the air-conditioner on. Bedlam House was quiet. We slipped down to the jetty and got into The Bedlam, rocking lazily beside The Lily of the West. Chick was back in her swimsuit, looking much happier.

'We'd better put on the sunscreen,' she said, 'and obey the Godfather!' We applied the stuff on each other—I had to be careful with her back. Then we put on our wide brimmed straw hats and took hold of the bright orange paddles. Of course, anyone on the beach or looking out from the verandahs could see us as we paddled across the lagoon, but that was fine and legal. Man, it was hard work. As we approached the northern extreme of the lagoon, I began looking ahead sharply. We had always assumed that the reef sort of ended at the tip of the northern pincer, but as we drifted along the inside of the reef, towards the pincer tip, it suddenly took a left turn heading straight out to sea. Then again, there was a right turn, curving around the pincer tip, just as I had spotted from the top of the tower. We paddled along slowly, our eyes shining. Once we took the right turn, we would no longer be visible from the beach, though legally we were still in a permitted zone in the lagoon. So, no dire law was being broken—just yet.

'Wow!' Chick said, resting her paddle, 'Just imagine, it's been under our noses all these years and we never knew!'

Then I spotted it—the sandy cove, tucked beneath the base of the tower and hidden from direct view above because of a rocky overhang.

'There! That's the landing spot!'

We scrunched softly onto the tiny beach, dragged The Bedlam onto the sand, and then looked around. The sand was silvery gold and scrunched pleasantly beneath our feet. The water was clear and bespangled; we could see shells and starfish rocking to and fro at the bottom as we waded out. The massive turret tower rose directly above us, gaunt and brooding. But there was a rocky path running around its base.

'That way!' Chick pointed. The 'path' was narrow and rocky as it hugged the base of the tower. We came around the curve and there to our right, was an opening in the tower wall—an alternative entrance to the base of the tower, which we had missed because rocks blocked it from the channel. Ahead, the path ended abruptly at the wall that had the tunnel we had come through earlier that morning.

'Man, we could have really saved ourselves some trouble this morning had we known this!' Chick said, 'But then, we never dreamed we could get here by boat too.'

'Better late than never!' I said 'So, this is how people reached the tower.'

'And if they were cut off by seaborne enemies, they just went through the tunnel and swam across to the other side. Of course they'd need to have a rope dangling down to get up the pincer though to access the lava field.'

'Aslam is going to hop with excitement when we tell him!'

She gave me a look. 'Sure, we'll tell him, but not about Romeo and Juliet!'

'Who?' I asked, momentarily horrified.

'Those two up there!'

'Oh, them! Want to go up to the tower again?'

'No,' she said, looking at the sapphire and emerald pool. 'I'd love to swim here but my back will start stinging again in the salt water.'

'Yeah, it looks like you've been in a clinch with Count Dracula!'

'Let's go back to that lovely cove.'

We lounged about in the cove for a while; lying on our towels on the soft sand.

'I wonder how many poor shipwrecked lovers have been stranded here,' Chick suddenly murmured, back in mush mode.

'Whatever. But this is a great place to hang out in. We can make a fire, cook stuff, mess about...'

'And camp here at night! That would be so cool!' She had the leopard glint back in her eyes. 'Can you imagine? We could come out, paddle over here, camp and sneak back home before dawn! Aslam could bring his mini-keyboard and we could jam!'

'He'd probably scare away those two up in the tower!' I retorted. Chick gave a snort of laughter and glanced up at the tower. I hooded my eyes and looked at her. The sun had illuminated her ears bright pink and gilded her long limbs. Her dragonfly earrings shot rainbow lasers as the sun caught it. A halo of pure gold outlined her body and set that nutcase French roll topknot ablaze. Dead cool.

By and by, we paddled back. The Lily of the West was no longer in her berth.

'Looks as if Dr D has gone sailing,' I remarked. The boathouse guy told us that both he and Mridula memsahib had left together. For a change, Bedlam House was quiet.

'Well that was quite a day!' I remarked as we entered the lobby.

'Yes,' Chick agreed. 'But I keep wondering what happened to Romeo and Juliet...' she said, 'Poor kids!'

We didn't know it then, but our grand plans for camping in the cove were going to be royally derailed. Because what happened that night swept the Romeo and Juliet skeletons out of our minds completely, much as a rip tide sweeps away careless swimmers from a beach.

3

J turned in early that night—it had been a pretty hectic, physical kind of day.

Till today, I still don't know what awoke me at 0118 hours that night—I suddenly found myself sitting bolt upright in bed. A cool sea breeze blew in from the verandah doors and windows. In the adjoining bed, Sohail slept with his arms and legs all over the place. Silently, I got up and padded out into the moonlit verandah. The nearly full moon hung in the night sky like a shiny silver medallion, turning the sea to heaving muscles of ink and mercury. The breeze was hushing through the casuarinas and fanning my brow. I went and stood at the railing—a guy needed a little time to chew the cud and think, and to watch the pinprick lights of ships slowly moving across the horizon. A cigarette, with its pulsating orange flare and rising coil of blue smoke would have been the ideal companion, but I knew the consequences of that could be catastrophic. I looked northwards, towards the looming black bulk of the turret tower in the distance, and wondered uneasily about the skeletons we had unearthed.

Who had they been? And now that we had disturbed them, would they come after us and haunt us? Nothing better than a night like this to do so—and something had woken me all right. But we'd left them in peace. Even so, had they put some sort of curse on us? And what had happened in the channel, that rogue wave—had that been an attempt on my life (if not dignity)? I could have been swept away if Chick hadn't grabbed me. And when she slid down the rock face she could have easily ripped open the back of her head on the rocks and given herself a fatal brain injury. Were those assassination attempts or mere warnings to us to stay away? I walked up to the end of our verandah, to the wall that partitioned it from the verandah in Chick's flat on the other side, and peered around it. Often, at night, we stood here after everyone had gone to bed and chatted quietly and could even pass stuff (usually snacks) to one another around the wall. Her verandah was in darkness, only the houseplants rustled gently in the breeze. (Dr D had once spotted us and had winked at us the next morning, murmuring, 'Ah, so I saw you two exchanging sweet nothings last night! It was very romantic, my dears!') Tonight, Chick must have been fagged out with all the stuff we had done today. I yawned—time to turn in.

Idly, I glanced at the sea—and stiffened. Just beyond the reef, a boat without lights was bobbing up and down amidst the faintly phosphorescent breakers. It was heading for the lagoon. I brought out my heavy duty Soviet-made 20X50 binoculars (a gift from Aslam's dad) and focused. Yes, there it was, now nosing carefully via the narrow zigzag channel through the reef, entering our bay—a white boat.

On just one such night (though I don't know if it had been a full moon one), terrorists had sailed into Mumbai undetected by anyone, to carry out their dastardly deeds. I glanced at the luminous dial of my watch. It was getting past 0130 hours. I looked up again. The boat was now through the channel and in the lagoon, and I thought I could hear the throbbing heartbeat of its engine. I focused on it again and breathed a sigh of relief.

It was a boat I knew only too well—The Lily of the West. The Dubashes were returning after their evening out—they must have gone for dinner to Mumbai. A fuse had probably blown, which was why they had no lights. Sure enough, the boat headed for the jetty at the southern tip and suddenly, the engine cut off and she was gliding silently in. The boat bumped against the jetty and I saw Dr D, his bald head gleaming in the moonlight, step off and fasten it. He was, oddly, dressed in a dark T-shirt and jeans. Then I stiffened again.

Four people, in hoodies and baggy black tunics, got off the boat, lugging aluminium cases; rather like the ones photographers use to carry big lenses. One fellow was well-built, probably six-feet tall, one stocky and two about as tall as Mridula Aunty. They had knapsacks on their backs. I couldn't tell how many amongst them were men and how many (if any) women. Behind them, Mridula Aunty followed, also dressed in dark jeans and a black top. The little group walked along the beach, disappearing from sight beneath the cliff. Suddenly, they emerged at the top of the steps to the garden gate. Here, they put the cases down and rested for a while to catch their breath. The well-built fellow turned to look at Bedlam House and I gasped. His face was covered too; I could just discern the silver pinpoints in his dark pupils peering through the eye slit. The stocky guy turned and embraced Dr D who hugged him back and then patted his back. One by one, they all turned to look at Bedlam House—their faces were covered. I quickly ducked below the verandah railings to avoid detection.

Then, I called Chick—she took ages to pick up, but she did.

'What the heck is the matter with you?' she asked irritably. 'Do you know the time?'

'Shut up, Lambu. Look out of the verandah. We have visitors—our godparent landlords have just turned up in their boat with four strangers carrying metal cases that could contain

AK-47s and grenades and RPGs. Babe, this is like a replay of 26/11!'

'Oh, stop talking rubbish and go back to sleep. Have you been drinking your dad's scotch? And don't "babe" me!'

'Just look out and then tell me.'

She did.

'So, what's so great about that?' she asked sleepily, 'Maybe it's just some friends or house guests they're having over; or those secret writer and poet people.'

'In the dead of night? Carrying suspicious knapsacks and heavy metal cases? Dressed like that? Are you serious?'

'Well, I'm going back to bed,' she grumbled. 'You snoop around all you want. If they shoot you, then we'll know, won't we? Why don't you take Aslam?'

'He's out of town, remember?' I said. 'So, are you coming?'

'Umm...' I could hear her yawn.

'It's exactly this kind of casual attitude that let the Mumbai terrorists get in, remember that! We have to be vigilant at all times. These are dark days!' I said direly.

Chick snorted. 'You think they're terrorists? You're nuts! They're with the *Dubashes*, for god's sake! Who give us tetanus shots and soothing ointments for scratches and teach bad puppies to be good! They *care*!'

And that's when the thunderbolt hit me. My eureka moment!

'Nitu, don't you see? The Annex! That's what they're using it for! A safe house for terrorists! That's what it's always been used for. It all fits in—it's like eureka!'

'So, are you going to run around naked yelling that?' she asked sweetly. 'If you are, count me out. I've already seen you once like that today! Besides, you'll get your head blown off for sure, which will be so nice!'

'See you in the driveway in five,' I said, succinctly ignoring her jibe. 'Be there!'

'Huh!' she snorted, 'You talk like some B-rated Hollywood wannabe.' But I knew she'd be there. She was one hell of a nosy parker.

I disconnected and looked out again. Not a soul in sight. The garden was empty. The party had vanished. Making sure I didn't wake Sohail, I collected my backpack and looked up and down the corridor outside the rooms. The parents' bedroom was at the other end of the corridor, its door firmly shut. I was down the verandah creeper (and drainpipe) in three minutes, wincing as the cuts in my hand protested and hoping that Night wouldn't start barking as I passed the Dubashes' floor. He didn't. After the immediate relief, it struck me odd that he hadn't already started to bark—surely he would have heard the boat's engine murmuring over the water and the people entering the garden?

'Hsst...you're white as a ghost!' Chick whispered sibilantly in my ear, making me jump. She grinned. I looked sceptically at her.

'So, where are these terrorists of yours?' she asked. She was dressed in denim shorts and a strappy loose white top that looked like it was made of cheesecloth. Her shoulders were bare. Her long thick single plait swung behind her like an elephant's tail. 'Let's take them out, Bozo!'

'My guess is that they're heading for the Annex. Remember, the last tenants there vacated a month ago—and we saw Mridula Aunty cleaning it up just this morning!' I looked tersely at her. 'Those people who stayed there last—we never even really saw who they were. They just came and went like smoke...' I narrowed my eyes. 'Did you have to wear white?'

'Bozo, I've been sleeping on my tummy barebacked. This is

the only thing that doesn't chafe against those cuts!'

'Oh, but not exactly camouflage, is it? You stick out like a beacon.'

'So, what do you want to do now?' Chick asked, yawning.

'We go to the tree house and watch the Annex from there. I've got my bins...'

'You know what's funny?' Chick said as we crept northwards along the lower garden towards the tree house. 'Night hasn't started yelling his head off!'

'Well, that's easy,' I said scornfully. 'Mridula Aunty is a dog trainer and must have tranquillizers. She must have drugged the poor fellow, so that he sleeps soundly while they creep in and get on with their nefarious activities.'

Chick just raised her eyebrows.

'Bozo,' she said suddenly, 'if they've gone to the Annex, the Dubashes must have gone with them to show them the way. They'll leave them there and return—and bump right into us if they do!'

Chick was right.

'We'll go through the casuarinas,' I said, veering across the lawn. 'They won't come through there.' We moved cautiously. A light was on in one of the Dubashes rooms, probably their bedroom, though otherwise Bedlam House was in darkness. The chowkidars must have been sleeping as usual.

'There!' Chick said, suddenly grabbing my hand and pointing. 'Look, they are returning!' From the cover of the casuarinas, we watched as the Dubashes walked back to the house. It was a close call and I kicked myself—I should have thought of it first. We continued on our way. We skirted the pond and made our way through the playground to the tree house.

'Here we are. Let's get up!' We climbed up and crawled in to take our positions at the Annex-facing 'windows.'

'It's all dark,' Chick commented. 'No lights are on in the Annex.'

'Maybe they're under blackout orders…'

She suddenly grabbed my arm. 'You're right,' she hissed excitedly. 'Look there—a flickering light. Someone's in the Annex, moving around with a lantern or candle or torch.'

'I told you,' I said triumphantly. 'Should we call the cops?'

Her eyes widened with scorn. 'Are you nuts? And tell them what—that the Dubashes have brought strangers who are probably terrorists to their home in the middle of the night? We have no proof of anything. They could be friends or relatives or nutcase artists—everyone knows the Dubashes are half wacko anyway and quite capable of doing such barmy things. Mridula Aunty also happens to train the cops' canine squad and knows them all well. They'll just laugh at us.'

She was right.

'Well, then we need proof,' I said.

'And how do you propose to get that?' Chick asked me sweetly. 'Knock on the door and ask whoever opens it, "Hey, hold your fire, but are you all here so you can shoot up another town?"'

Chick can be a hell of a pain in the butt sometimes.

I looked at her and grinned. 'Actually, that's more up your street—why don't you try that? Just walk up, ring the bell and say, "Hi, welcome! We're your neighbours. We just wanted to say hello and ask you your life story and what you want to blow up!"'

'Very funny!' she snorted. Then she said, 'Say, did you brush your teeth after dinner? Sure smells like you didn't! You must have eaten a lot of raw onions and garlic! Eww!' Suddenly, she clutched at me again.

'Hey, look, they've switched on the lights now—both upstairs and downstairs!'

But the curtains drawn across the rooms were dark and heavy and we could only make out vague shadows moving behind them. We stared for a while—there were two figures moving upstairs and two downstairs. Then, within the next few minutes, the lights went out.

'So, what's our plan of action?' I asked her. 'What should we do?'

'Well I'm going to bed,' she said. 'We know there are new tenants who have arrived in a rather unconventional manner in the middle of the night. We can start snooping around tomorrow.'

'Don't ask Mridula Aunty or Dr D any leading questions!' I warned. 'They might suspect we know and then...'

She shook her head. 'I don't really believe they would be involved in anything like that,' she said. 'I mean Dr D looks after little kids and Mridula Aunty teaches naughty doggies to be good...'

'The perfect cover, don't you think? Who on earth would suspect them? And they've got the perfect landing spot—the beach below and safe house nearby. No one comes here. They usher in the hostiles under the cover of darkness in their own boat, and keep them here. Maybe they're just 'sleepers' waiting for the signal to attack, and when they get that, they just vanish to carry out their dastardly deeds. Maybe they come back here to escape the same way they came!' My eyes suddenly widened and I thumped my fist into my palm. 'If you recall the conversation we overhead this morning when Dr D was treating you...something about laying low and meeting at CST. That must be Chhatrapati Shivaji Station—Victoria Terminus! They picked them up from there and brought them here! Man, oh, man!'

Chick just raised her eyebrows and yawned. Girls, I tell you!

'Or,' she said sleepily, 'if they're suicide bombers, they won't come back at all after their mission!'

'Tell you what!' I said. 'We'll have a meeting here tomorrow afternoon to decide an action plan on how to get evidence. Aslam should be back by midday!'

It's funny how your suspicions fade away in daylight. I found myself having serious doubts about what we, well, I, had concluded last night. I steeled myself—this was exactly the sort of psychological mindset people like terrorists took advantage of. We'd better make sure one way or the other. We needed proof of their innocence; or otherwise. Being in limbo was not an option.

Aslam and his family returned by lunchtime the next day. I apprised him of what we had discovered the previous day; about both the access to the turret tower and what had happened last night.

He whistled long and low. 'No way, man! You guys have been busy! So, what's our POA (plan of action)?'

'We make one this afternoon—tree house at 1500 hours! Be there!'

'Will do, boss!'

At 2.30 p.m., he rang again. 'Can't make it, boss! My parents had to rush off to town. Some friend is in the hospital. Amma still hasn't come back from leave. I have to babysit Sari!'

Shoot. We could meet at his place, but I wanted to put the Annex under surveillance as soon as possible. For that, we had to be at the tree house.

'Bring her along. Lambu can take care of her!'

At 2.45 p.m., just as I was trying to sneak out, I found I had a problem too.

'Bhaiyya, where are you going?' Sohail popped his head up sleepily from his bed, rubbing his eyes. 'I want to come too!'

'Well, you can't! It's too hot and Mama says you have to sleep!'

'Are you going to the tree house? I'm coming with you, bhaiyya. Or I'll tell Mama you are going!'

'Nitu didi will be there and she'll pinch your cheeks all the time!' I warned.

'Doesn't matter! I'll pinch her back.' He had begun putting on his shoes.

Dammit. He was like a leech. He wouldn't let go. And I was getting late. 'Okay, come along. Take your hat and shut up!'

We went down. The lobby was silent and empty. I rang Chick. 'I'm on my way, in the lobby! Be down in three!'

She yawned on the phone. 'Hullo? Oh, I'm so sleepy! Don't feel like it...'

'Lambu, this could be a matter of national security!'

'Bozo, you read too much garbage.'

'Besides, Aslam's coming, and he has to bring Sari along. And I have baggage too—Sohail is tagging along with me!'

'How the heck is Aslam going to get Sari up the tree house?' She was suddenly alert.

'He'll carry her up somehow.' I said.

'Listen, don't you let him take a step up that ladder with that baby!' she suddenly yelled, wide awake. 'Not till I get there! You guys are such morons! See you in five!'

'Copy that!' I said, disconnecting. I glared at Sohail. 'Nitu's coming right now and she's really going to pinch your cheeks!'

'Bhaiyya!'

Aslam was pacing up and down at the base of the tree house when we got there. He's just a fraction taller than I am, wiry and rather like a ferret in his movements; always looking for quick getaway routes. His eyes are black and sharp and twinkling and always scanning for trouble. His ears, well, they're pretty widescreen; his hair lank and inky blue-black. Sarika was asleep in her stroller. Aslam kept looking at the dangling rope ladder and the baby, obviously trying to figure out a way to get her up.

'Hi boss, hey So!' he greeted us as we walked up to him. He looked at his sister and grimaced. 'How do we get her up? I tried carrying her with one hand and nearly dropped her; the damn ladder began rotating.'

'Lambu's just coming. She'll find a way.' I raised my eyebrows. 'Or she can remain down here with her and Sohail while we go up...'

Chick loped along within minutes. She made a face. 'Thank god you didn't try anything silly like carry her up with one hand,' she said. Aslam and I exchanged glances.

'So, any bright ideas on how we can get her up?' I asked.

'Easy!' She delved into her rucksack, which she had slung over her shoulder, and pulled out a funny blue bag-like thing.

'What the heck is that?'

'A baby carrier! It's what mom used to carry me around in— don't you remember? You strap it to your back or your front and put the baby into it.'

Aslam grinned. 'Righto, great.' He bent over to pick up his sister.

'Hey, hang on, buster. You're the one who's going to carry her!' Chick said as Aslam turned to her in surprise. 'She's your little sister and anyway my back is scratched to ribbons!'

Carefully, we 'papoosed' poor Aslam and then Lambu put

Sari into the pouch.

'Okay?' she asked, grinning. She kissed the baby.

'Hmph!' The baby was still asleep. 'Up you go, carefully now!' We watched as he climbed up and disappeared inside.

Then I made Sohail go up and we followed him up to the tree house.

'Okay, the meeting will come to order,' I said, immediately aware that we had another problem. I glanced at Sohail. We'd have to talk in riddles so that he wouldn't understand what we were saying, or he'd go and blab it all out to Ma and Dad.

'We have become aware of certain developments and need to...to err...make certain observations...'

'Hey Sohail, can I pinch your cheeks just once?' Chick asked as I glared at her.

Sohail made for the farthest corner of the tree house and hid behind a cushion. I lowered my voice.

'And we need to continue making those observations until the time we've made enough to take action.'

Chick grinned and Aslam glanced towards the Annex. I nodded furtively.

'What sort of action are you thinking of, boss?' he asked.

'It could be direct, it could be indirect, it'll depend on the evidence we gather.'

'And how do we do that?'

I glanced again at Sohail. He'd settled himself down amidst the cushions and his eyes were closing. He'd be asleep in minutes. I nodded faintly in his direction.

'Okay,' I said in a low voice. 'He's asleep. We can talk...'

'So do you really think there are terrorists holed up there in the Annex?' Aslam asked, his eyes sparkling.

'Bozo really thinks so, I'm not so sure,' Chick said. 'But yes, they came by boat in the middle of the night and were oddly dressed; all covered up!'

'Let's just go and knock on their door and see who opens it,' Aslam said.

'And what excuse do we give for knocking on their door? We can hardly say, "Hi, we just wanted to see what you look like and ask if you have any guns and bombs in your bags!"' I said sarcastically.

'Easy, boss—we play cricket, the ball goes into their lawn; we knock on the door to kindly ask them if we can retrieve it...' Aslam shrugged, grinning.

'Hey look, they're still there!' Chick said, suddenly. She'd been looking at the Annex through the bins. 'Two people just came out into the balcony; their mouths and faces are still covered! Oh shoot, they've gone back in already.'

I thought about Aslam's plan—it seemed good, perfectly feasible. I nodded.

'Okay, we'll do that. We'll play in the driveway just outside the gate.' A gravel drive led from Bedlam House to the gates of the Annex.

'I still don't believe the Dubashes can be involved in something like this,' Chick said, shaking her head.

'Well, you saw as well as I did what happened last night.'

'There's got to be some simple explanation.'

'Well, maybe we'll know soon.'

'So, when do we play our game?'

'This evening? Say around five? Okay, we're done here now. Reconvene at 1700 hours with equipment.' We went back to Bedlam House. Aslam charged off home (his mom was hollering for him) and I turned to Chick as we stood outside our respective front doors.

'Say, how's the back?'

'Much better, Bozo! The scabs are forming—it's a bit itchy, that's all.'

'Good!'

'And your hands?'

'They're fine!'

A police bus drove into Bedlam House at 1700 hours and just for a moment I thought the cops had been tipped off about the terrorists. Maybe, just maybe, the Dubashes had lured the terrorists into the Annex last night and then ratted on them. Maybe they were counter-insurgents, or secretly working for intelligence.

A bunch of excited, shiny German shepherds alighted from the bus with their handlers and made for the lower garden, their tails wagging like mad. From the house, Night came gamboling down to meet his elite friends. From Chick's verandah, Cushion yapped shrilly. The cops and their dogs lined up as Mridula Aunty emerged, smiling, and greeted the fellow in charge. She was in jeans and a denim jacket.

Aslam and I (along with Sohail) waited for Chick in the lobby with our cricket stuff—bats, tennis ball and wickets. We watched as Mridula Aunty began her session. These were not the sniffer dogs; these were crowd and crime control attack dogs. One of the cops was strapping on a massive amount of padding to his arm. The handlers and their dogs stood at the far edge of the garden, near the fence. Suddenly, the padded cop began running for leather. One of the handlers gave a sharp command and released his young German shepherd. The silly fellow barked delightedly and ran up to Night and began playing, ignoring the fleeing criminal. A couple of the other dogs began barking ferociously.

'All right, take Sheru back, he's very new to all this,' Mridula Aunty laughed. She pointed to one of the other constables. 'Let Rocky show him what has to be done.'

Sheru was hauled back and made to sit. The padded cop ran again. Rocky's handler let go his dog with a sharp command. The German shepherd took off after the man barking ferociously. Within moments, he had sprung, bringing the man down and worrying his padded arm, growling and snarling.

'*Chhodo*! Leave him!' the handler barked, running up to the man. The dog obeyed, but stood near the poor padded cop, making sure he didn't move.

'Shabash! Well done!'

We could watch these dogs all evening, but we had our own mission.

'I wouldn't like to have one of those dogs come after me,' Chick said, as she joined us.

Well, cricket didn't quite work out the way we imagined. Tried as we did, the damn ball just refused to bounce into the Annex garden.

'Okay,' I said at last, getting fed up. 'Let's try French cricket. We'll bat facing the gate, so any straight shot will head towards the garden.'

And within five minutes, Chick had thwacked the ball high and long, straight at the Annex. It bounced into the first-floor verandah and disappeared.

'You're out!' we yelled. 'You hit it out of bounds.'

She glared at us (she'd been batting damn well). 'Well, let's go and retrieve it,' she said.

In a group, we walked slowly up the driveway. This was the

second time for me and the first for the others, but man, this time it was worse than the Navy Seals entering Osama's lair. They had been armed to the teeth—we only had two cricket bats.

'We'll ring the bell on the ground floor first,' Chick said, sotto voce, tying up her hair as if getting ready for action. 'We'll pretend that the ball is somewhere in the garden. Then, we'll go up!'

Aslam rang the bell.

We shifted uneasily, the tension rising. This was it. Would someone open the door with an Uzi or AK-47 pointed at us?

'Get behind me,' I muttered to the others. I was the boss; if there was a hit I had to take the first shots.

I shoved Sohail behind me, but the others just flanked me, ignoring the command. Silence—I was just about to ring again when I heard soft footfalls. Aslam pointed at the peephole. An eye had appeared. We heard the sound of bolts being drawn and then slowly, the latch twisted—the door creaked open gradually.

The tall and saturnine-looking man opened the door. His nose and mouth were covered with a black cloth. He was wearing a black tunic and jeans. His eyes, like beads of tar, darted suspiciously across us.

'*Hanji?* Yes?' he asked softly. 'What do you want?'

'O…our…ball…' we stuttered. Then Chick smiled at him.

'Uncle, our ball came into the garden. Can we look for it?'

He looked relieved and nodded. '*Zaroor* (Sure)!'

'Thank you, Uncle.'

We trooped back into the garden and began searching for the ball. The man shut the door. After five or ten minutes, we gathered together again, pretending to look puzzled.

'Not here; where the hell is it?' I said, looking around, perplexed.

'Bhaiyya, but it's in the balcony upstairs,' Sohail tattled in his high clear voice. 'It went there, I saw it!' I glared at him.

'Shut up! It must have bounced down after that! It's got to be here somewhere.'

'Hey, maybe, he's right,' Lambu said loudly, pinching Sohail and smiling. 'Maybe it is stuck upstairs.'

'Let's go up and ask!' said Aslam.

I nodded. The steps leading to the flat above led from outside the ground floor flat. But this was going to be really dangerous—to access the verandah, we'd have to pass through the house, at least the living and dining rooms. We trooped upstairs.

The guy who opened the door seemed damn nervous and jumpy. He had, for god's sake, pulled a green monkey cap down over his face!

'Yes, yes,' he squeaked in a high-pitched voice, 'what do you want?'

'Uncle, we think our ball may have landed in the balcony. Could we check, please?' Chick asked sweetly. At her side, Sohail nodded.

'Yes, I saw it!'

'Oh!' the fellow looked nonplussed. Then, another figure, one of the smaller ones, also clad in a black tunic and face covered, appeared beside him. A woman—her hands were fair and her glass bangles clinked. Her eyes were huge, dark and worried. She looked at the man nervously.

'Okay, I will go and check,' he said and turned. Before he could shut the door, Chick did something crazy. She put out her hand, pushed the door wide open and walked inside after him.

'Uncle, we'll help you,' she offered smiling, 'sometimes it gets stuck in the rain gutter and that's difficult to reach, but we have our bats!' We swaggered in behind her, bumping against each other. We were in the terrorists' lair! The woman's eyes widened and the man looked momentarily stunned. Then he recovered and beckoned us to follow him. My eyes got used to the dimness of the corridor and flickered around. The living room and dining room were also dim, because all the curtains had been drawn. No sign of any weapons or cases: they were probably in the bedroom. There were fruits on the dining table—bananas and oranges and mangoes. When the hell did they go shopping for fruits? Or had Mridula Aunty supplied them?

And there were also papers—dark blue Indian passports and official-looking documents. Most tellingly, a map of Mumbai spread open over half the table! Holy crap! What the heck were these guys hatching?

The man unbolted the verandah door and we went out. Sure enough, the yellow ball was reposing in a corner.

'Found it!' I said exultantly, pouncing on it.

The man nodded. 'Good!'

'Uncle, are you and aunty staying long?' Chick asked, smiling sweetly. Got to say, sometimes it's useful having a chick around for the small talk.

The man shook his head and smiled briefly. 'No, very short time,' he mumbled.

'Oh, but it's so beautiful here, isn't it?'

The fellow nodded. I went up close to Chick, my eyes hooded.

'We need to access the bedroom,' I whispered to her. She didn't make as if she'd heard me. Then, she suddenly looked sharply at Sohail.

'Baba, I think you need to go to the bathroom, don't you?' she said, as Sohail looked surprised. We all did. 'Uncle, can I take him to the bathroom, please?'

'But, Didi...'

In a second, I got what Chick was up to. Got to say, brilliant!

'Sohail, you do as didi says,' I ordered, pushing him firmly forward. 'Go and do *susu*!'

'But...but...'

'Come on, now!' Chick took his hand. The man and woman hesitated and then opened the bedroom door.

'Thank you, he's just a little fellow!'

'I'm not!' But Chick and I had propelled him into the bedroom and towards the bathroom. 'We'll be right outside. Do *susu*, use the flush and wash your hands!' I barked, shoving him into the bathroom. We half-closed the door and glanced around quickly. The room was tidy: the bed made, the chairs and tables neatly arranged, even sunflowers in a vase, a copy of *Outlook* on one bedside table. These guys' housekeeping was up to scratch. But the man and the woman had been completely taken aback by our attack; the fellow smiled nervously and the woman wrung her hands. I did wonder—hardened terrorists would hardly be nervous. Maybe this was their first assignment; or maybe we had caught them unawares and unarmed. Suddenly, I noticed that Aslam had not come into the bedroom. Good man!

'Little boys,' Chick prattled on as if she was 35 or something. 'They hold on till the last minute and then...' She rolled her eyes. I raked the room again.

Four aluminium cases—two metallic pink, two silver; one not shut properly and with what looked like clothes sticking out— and two heavy looking olive-green (army issue?) rucksacks were stacked in one corner on the floor. But there was no signs of any arms or ammunition. I would have given my ears to have been able to open the cases.

Sohail emerged and Chick promptly went into the bathroom.

'I'll just check he's flushed and not left a mess,' she explained glibly.

In the living room, Aslam waited for us, twitching impatiently and looking like the cat that had eaten the canary.

And then, we were safely out, almost tripping over each other in our haste to get down the stairs. If they had suspected anything, this would be the moment bullets would slam into our backs.

'Tree house right away,' I ordered as we headed to the playground.

'So, what did you see in the bathroom?' I asked Chick. She shrugged.

'Nothing unusual. Two toothbrushes, toothpaste—a small Close-up, a shaving kit, handwash, towels, shower gel...some clothes drying on the shower curtain rail.'

'Damn!'

It seemed we still had no incriminating evidence.

Only we did.

I looked at Chick and Aslam and then glanced at Sohail. Before anything else, we had to get rid of little Big Ears here. Chick grinned wickedly.

'Heh heh, Sohail baba!' she sang, deepening her already husky voice. 'Now I got you where I want you! Come and sit in my lap, baba,' she reached out to him. 'Then I can cuddle you and pinch you and smother you with kisses all evening! So come along now!'

Sohail looked appalled and backed away rapidly.

Aslam and I grinned mercilessly. 'Sohail and Nitu, sitting in a tree! Kay Eye Ess Ess I n g!' I chanted. Sohail looked like he was going to burst into tears.

'I'm going to tell Mama!' he yowled, heading for the doorway. 'And I'm going to tell Mridula Aunty to set the dogs on you!'

'Hey wait a sec, hero,' I said going to the doorway. 'I go down first then you follow...you know the rules!' I slithered down and watched, as sniffing, he came down. He glared at me, his face red, and stomped off towards Bedlam House. I watched him go and then went up. I knew he'd quickly get distracted and spend his time happily watching the dogs—no problem really.

'Poor fellow,' Chick said, 'I feel so bad! I'll have to make him some brownies to make up!'

'Okay, back to matters at hand,' I said, 'like I was about to say—we do have evidence! If those guys were here only for a short time, why would they need to carry so much luggage? Four suitcases and two big rucksacks—just for two people on a short trip? Doesn't make sense to me.'

Aslam grinned and took his phone out of his pocket. 'Boss, I took these when you all were in the bedroom,' he said. 'Couldn't do both passports though...' he added apologetically.

He'd flipped open one of the passports and photographed the first pages; as well as one of the papers.

The passport was made out in the name of one Shri Ashok Chauhan; Father's name: Sharad Chauhan; DOB: 31/01/1994; Place of birth: Saharanpur (UP).

There was an address (can't reveal that here, it's confidential); Date of expiry was 31/01/2020; Passport No.: Well that's confidential too—even if the entire identity is fake anyway.

The single sheet that he had photographed was an Air India e-ticket for a flight to New York. Date of Boarding: Exactly a week ahead.

My heart started pounding again and I went pale. An Air India ticket... Maybe they all had air tickets... Maybe these guys were going to try something like 9/11 all over again. Once on board they could crash the plane wherever they wanted, en route Mumbai, London, New York, or even hijack it to Delhi and crash it on the House of Parliament. But then, why all that luggage? Why carry bombs if you wanted to crash a plane? Well, maybe they didn't know how to fly and would simply explode the bombs after hijacking the plane… Or…or maybe they'd put the bombs in places all over Mumbai, set to go off a day after they'd taken off for New York themselves. The theories swilled around in my head.

I looked at the photo—an ordinary looking young man, fairly tanned, with curly black hair and a beard. He had a blank expression, looking slightly nervous, if anything; no selfie grin here. Nothing really menacing about it. He didn't look like the 'typical' terrorist, but who did? Just another youth like millions in the country.

'We can Google this or check out Facebook and Twitter,' I said. 'We might find something.'

Aslam's eyes glittered. 'We could ring Air India and warn them…and tip off the cops.'

'We could! Though I doubt they'd find any evidence—except when the bombs go off later… It would nail them, but the damage would have been done, and anyway, they'd probably blow themselves up once they realize the game was up.'

'Man this is deep, real deep!'

'Bozo,' Chick said, 'so far, we still have no concrete evidence. Apart from the fact that they turned up in the middle of the night and dress oddly, and may be leaving for New York next week, we have zilch! Maybe they're just here on a holiday…'

'Then why the hoodies and all the hush-hush intrigue? When we walked in, I half expected them to take out AK-47s and empty them into us.'

'Boss! That would have blown their cover! For them, the mission is paramount!'

'Well,' Chick said, 'if as you think they're going to plant bombs all over Mumbai, they'll have to go there first. So, let's see if they do!'

'That means a stake-out!'

'Great, man! Yeah, we can take turns keeping watch from here!' Aslam's eyes shone.

I hooded my eyes. 'Guys, it's gotta be 24×7! No point in us going home in the evening and them take off at night...'

'So, when do we begin the stake-out?' Aslam asked, 'Right now?'

I shook my head. 'I don't think they'd plant the bombs so early. There'd be a high risk of them being discovered. Today's what? Friday... So their flight is next Friday, which means they'll probably start planting the bombs on next Thursday. With a one-day buffer, in case something doesn't work out.'

'Wow, you've got this all neatly taped, haven't you?' Chick said, her eyebrows up again.

'I read,' I said coldly. 'I read stuff. And you've got to think like them.'

'Well,' she said sweetly, 'if you read the papers today, you'd know that the prime minister is visiting Mumbai next weekend...'

'Holy crap!'

'Bingo!'

'I think,' Chick went on in that smarmy tone of hers, 'I think if they are who you think they are, that's what they are waiting for...'

Smarmy or not, got to hand it to her; Chick was good—brilliant even, as I believe I said before.

'I think,' I said, slowly nodding my head, 'I think you might be on to something there.'

'Bozo,' she said sweetly, reaching out and pinching my cheek, 'I think so too!'

4

𝒯ell you, man, I couldn't sleep that night. I just didn't like it one bit. Out there, in the Annex, not so far away were at least eight suitcases and four rucksacks, probably crammed with high explosives, and we could do nothing about them just yet. I rang Chick.

'What now?' she asked irascibly, 'More terrorists arriving tonight?'

'Listen, we can't wait around,' I said, 'we've just got to see what's in those suitcases. We can take photos and then tip off the cops. We can't wait till the last moment.'

'And how do you propose we do that?'

'We'll have to think of something.' My mind churned furiously. 'Listen, that map of Mumbai was lying open on the dining table. Maybe they were checking out the hotspots—places where to plant the bombs...'

'So?'

'So maybe they will go to Mumbai to do a recce. A physical verification! Maybe we should stake-out the Annex from tomorrow itself. If we see them leave, then we can sneak in and check the bags. If they're going to Mumbai, they'll be gone at least the whole day. We'll have plenty of time!'

'Bozo, you read too much crap! But maybe you've got something there.'

'Of course!'

'How do you think they'll go? Call a radio cab?'

'We'll just stake-out and find out, won't we?'

'Well yeah, and get this, mom's going off on one of her Bharat Darshan tours and I have to shift to Mridula Aunty's place because daddy has to attend that annual bash they have at Lonavala every year.'

I nodded. 'Yes, mom and dad are going there too! But oh boy, that's great! You'll be like a mole in the enemy's camp. You can snoop around and find out more!'

'Yeah, and hack into Dr D's and Mridula Aunty's laptops, I guess,' Chick said, and I didn't really know if she was being sarcastic or serious. She was a whiz with computers after all.

'We should do the stake-out in pairs—so if one of us falls asleep, the other can wake him or her up.'

'There are three of us,' she pointed out, 'unless you want Sohail to join us too.'

'Are you kidding? Maybe Aslam can do his stint alone...' I grinned, 'He's still a bit girl-shy and you keep ragging him!'

'And you are not?'

'We'll give him shorter stints than ourselves; just an hour at a time. But it'll have to be 24×7.'

She snorted. 'Bozo, I doubt they'll leave in the middle of the night to do a recce. It'll be more sensible to set out by day— they'd be able to mingle with the crowd that way. If they're caught snooping around at night, well, that's asking for trouble.'

'You know what?' I said, 'You'll make a very good one of them!'

'Thank you.'

'Rendezvous in the lobby at 0650 hours tomorrow. I'll brief Aslam!' Suddenly, something else struck me. I rang her again.

'What now?' she asked irritably.

'Shut up and listen. If they leave during the day as you said, they'll hardly be all covered up and masked and what not. That'll be asking for trouble. They'll have to dress normally and we'll be able to see what they really look like. And maybe, we can click their pictures too, if we see them leave.'

'Bozo, sometimes, you can be quite smart,' Chick said in her usual sardonic way. 'See ya tomorrow morning. God—and I thought I'd be able to sleep in during these holidays.'

'It's in the national interest, Chick,' I said, sternly. 'Don't ever forget that!'

'Don't chick me, buster!'

I briefed Aslam and he said he'd meet us in the lobby at 0650. But he's a notorious late riser and there was no sign of him in the lobby at 0650 hours. Chick was there. Sohail, thank god, was getting a bit fed up of the tree house business and Lambu's teasing. We slipped away.

'We'll brief Aslam later,' I said impatiently. I wanted to be at the tree house as soon as I could. 'He takes ages to wake up.'

There was no activity around the Annex.

'When do you have breakfast?' I asked Chick.

'Around 8.30–9.'

'Same here! Tell you what, we'll tell Aslam to fill in that period. We'll stay here till around 8.30 and return after breakfast. I'll ring him now.'

'We'd better organize the timings properly,' she said. 'Otherwise there'll be chaos!'

'Sure! Bring whatever you need—music, iPad etc... We'll have to sit around for quite a while.'

'Yeah, and I've packed a case. I'll leave it at Mridula Aunty's place.'

'Great!'

'Your mom and dad trust you and Sohail enough to leave

you at home alone?' Chick asked, her eyes wide.

'No!' I grinned. 'They were thinking of taking Sohail with them to Lonavala. They think I can manage by myself. I guess I'll be eating my meals with you at Dr D's though.'

'So, only poor Aslam will be leashed!' she said with a grin. 'Poor guy!' His mom is one big tyrant, isn't she?'

'Well, at least the two of us will be more or less free!' I said. 'That's pretty cool.'

Have to say, we got things pretty well taped. Aslam turned up at 8.30 a.m., and Chick and I went back home for our breakfast and baths.

'Bhaiyya, what are you doing today?' Sohail asked.

'Going to the tree house. We're spending the whole day there.'

'Why?'

'Because it's fun to be up in the trees.'

'Will Nitu didi be there?'

'I guess.'

'Then I'm not coming.'

'Good!'

'But I'll be going to Lonavala!'

'Good.'

'And you're not coming!'

'No, I'm not.'

'I'm going to Lonalava, you're staying here! I'm going to…'

'I heard you!'

'I'll eat *chikki*, you won't!'

I was back at the tree house at 9.30 a.m., and I immediately relieved Aslam. Chick said she'd be there by 10.15. As I left for the tree house, I saw that Mridula Aunty was getting ready for another class.

'Aunty, are the police dogs coming again today?'

She smiled. 'No, there will only be regular pet dogs.'

It was pretty boring sitting up in the tree house alone. I fiddled with my tablet. I had already Googled and Twittered, Facebooked and YouTubed the name we had discovered in the passport, but none of the pictures or descriptions that popped up remotely resembled our terrorists. Besides, the identity was obviously fake, so it was pretty pointless. I couldn't see a film or play a game because that would distract me from my watch. From time to time, I raked the Annex with my bins, and thought I saw shadowy movements behind the thick curtains. The quarry was still holed up there!

Chick turned up at 10.20 a.m.—much to my relief.

'Hi, I told Aslam to relieve us at 1300 hrs. We'll go back for lunch. Suits him; he has to go for his music class. He said he didn't mind doing his stint alone.' Aslam was preparing for some tough piano exam.

'So we sit here and do nothing till then?' She didn't sound terribly enthusiastic.

I leant my head back against a cushion, hooded my eyes and appraised her. Suddenly it struck me—it would be a good training to observe her in detail, as I would, a suspect. In case I had to provide the authorities with a detailed description of her.

Unusually, Chick had kept her hair loose, and man, it was a lot of very thick shiny jet black hair, cascading way below her back, down to her waist. I'd rarely seen her with her hair open like this. She was wearing a long, droopy olive-green skirt and a sleeveless white top with olive green leaves all over it. I scanned her face—straight nose, small pink ears, with great silver hoops dangling from them, deep-set dark brown (or black?) eyes that held the glint of a hunting leopard (as you know, I like the sound of that!), a slender neck, long brown arms, with delicate (but strong) wrists and piano-player fingers, with short but pink glossed nails. Her teeth were even and white, eyebrows thick but tapering, with a few frown lines on her forehead. The white belt at her waist made her look lily-slender and softly curvy. She sat with her knees drawn up to her chin, flicking glances at me.

'What?' she asked, 'Why are you staring at me like that? As if I have warts! Or are you checking me out?'

'Not staring... But...your...your hair! Man!'

'I had to wash it again; all the sand didn't come out the first time. Thank god it's almost dry. It's quite a pain to look after. I'm thinking of cutting it.'

'Don't!' I blurted involuntarily and up went those eyebrows. 'Oh? Why?'

Because Chick had always had long hair, ever since I could remember. I couldn't imagine her without it; she wouldn't quite be Chick without it.

'Bec...because it's...it's like an elephant's tail!'

'Thanks! So, you like elephants' tails, eh? Now, what should we do?' she asked.

'Keep a watch on that house!'

'Bozo!'

'Okay, so we can play "I Spy"!'

We did for a bit and all through the game, I found my eyes flickering over her again. She was tall and gangly as a giraffe, yes, but her movements were graceful as a deer's—not awkward at all. And when she shifted up close to point out the jackfruit she had 'spied', I got rather distracted by the waterfall of perfumed silken hair that momentarily swished along my cheek and arm.

'You know what?' she said suddenly. 'I just had an idea...of how to speed this whole thing up...'

'Speed what up?'

'This stupid, boring stake-out. Why don't we go and make friends with them?'

'With whom?'

She jerked her firm chin towards the Annex. 'Them.'

'The enemy? How?'

'Very simple! We'll take them a tray of cookies or brownies and tell them we're sorry for having barged in that day...'

'They might just take the biscuits or whatever and slam the door in our faces.'

'They won't. We'll also ask for a drink of water. They'll have to call us in then.'

'Okay...so when?'

'This evening! We'll have to make the cookies first, remember. Listen, we'll make Aslam stay here in the afternoon and I'll come over to your place and bake them. He can bring his mini-keyboard here and practise or whatever.'

'Yeah, he has an exam coming up.'

'So we get in and then what?'

'We talk. We ask them where they're from, and why they've come and how they found out about the Annex, whether they'll be going sightseeing in Mumbai and other places, and what they want to see—innocent questions like that. If we can ask them separately, they may slip up and give us different answers. We'll ask questions that adults expect nosy kids to ask.' She looked at me and grinned, 'Or as you would say, we interrogate them!'

'Lambu, don't forget, they're probably hardened terrorists,

trained to kill without mercy, women and children included.'

'But not until they've accomplished their mission or think that they've been discovered.'

'It's hell of a risk!' But I liked the sound of it. Should have thought of it myself really; certainly better than sitting here twiddling our thumbs.

'It's in the national interest, Bozo. You said so yourself!'

'I guess.'

Suppose we did succeed in unraveling the terrorists' dastardly plan. We'd be national heroes! The whole country would salute us! We'd meet the PM (whose life we had obviously saved) and the president. We'd be VIP guests at the Republic Day parade. They'd name awards and roads after us.

'What are you dreaming about?' she asked. I glanced at her—those leopard eyes were fixed on me, glinting; there was a 'wicked witch' smile on her lips, and then there was the furrowing of her brows.

'Uh, nothing.'

'Hmm'. She took out a wooden hairbrush and began brushing her hair, till it was silken smooth and shining. Then, she grinned laconically at me.

'You like elephants' tails, don't you?'

'What?' I felt myself going red. That had been a bad slip up, I should watch my step (and mouth) in future.

'So, come and make one. Plait my hair, Bozo. I'll show you how...'

'Pl...plait your hair?' We were on a stake-out, watching out for terrorists who were planning to blow up half of Mumbai, and Chick wanted me to plait her hair! Told you, girls think of the daftest things.

'Yes, come on. It's not difficult... I'll show you! You start

from the top…divide it into three strands… Come on, sit here…
Now watch me…'

I watched with hawk's eyes—man, it was like doing that cat's cradle thing.

Then, she unravelled what she had braided.

'Okay, now, I'll place my hands over yours and guide your fingers.'

Her fingers interlocked with mine, guiding them through the silken strands of her hair, weaving them into a thick shiny rope.

Have to say, I got the hang of it pretty damn quick. Also, that lovely silken hair between my fingers felt real good. Her fingers now brushed mine lightly, just ensuring they were doing the right thing. And man, the scent was heady.

'Thanks, I love having my hair plaited by someone,' she murmured, taking the final thick twist of the plait and fixing it with a rubber band. 'Whatever else, you've got nimble fingers, Bozo! You'll make a great pickpocket.'

'Uh huh, thanks!'

Suddenly, she leaned her head back against my chest, just under my chin, rested it there for a moment and closed her eyes. I froze.

Holy moly! What was this? A cry for help? For protection? A mute appeal that she wasn't such a tough cookie after all and needed a guy to take care of her? Even just to braid her hair? That she wanted me to put my arms around her and tell her everything would be all right? Or was she just going mushy on me (all those books)? Or trying to mess with my head? The thoughts flashed through my brain like an electrical storm. Then she picked up a couple of bop-pins and fixed them in her hair. There was a wicked glint in her eyes.

She came over at 2.30 p.m., carrying a large tray with all the stuff we needed to put 'Operation Brownie' into action. I looked at her long, thick braid that I had made, and suddenly I felt as if I knew Chick better than I had ever before—that she'd let me into this personal space of hers; like a secret room. That she trusted me. It felt nice, but man, I was wary too. Had her head been messed up by the mush she had been reading?

Mom and dad had left for Lonavala about an hour earlier with Sohail. It felt good (and it was high time) that they trusted me home alone! I was to have my meals with the Dubashes.

'Now, don't burn the house down or anything like that!' Mom had warned. 'I've told Mridula Aunty to keep an eye on you, and also Aslam's mom.'

'Mom, I can look after myself!' I had said.

'Right!' Chick said, marching into the kitchen and flipping open a dog-eared notebook. 'I've brought all we need—cocoa, butter, sugar, flour and walnuts…now let's get cracking. You guys have a weighing scale somewhere here?'

I pulled it out.

'Okay, get out some sheets of paper. We'll pour the ingredients into them and weigh them. Okay, cocoa powder first. Um…60 grams. Got it? Now, 240 grams of sugar, 90 grams of flour and 165 grams of butter. That's just over one and a half flat-packs. Got it?'

'Hang on…'

'And walnuts—120 grams of chopped walnuts. Oh shoot! I forgot the eggs. You have eggs?'

'I guess.' I opened the fridge.

'We'll need two.' I took the eggs out.

'Okay, get a saucepan and put in six tablespoons of water...'

'What's a tablespoon—this?' I asked, pulling out a large spoon from the cutlery holder. She glared at me, pulled open a drawer and scanned the kitchen implements.

'Here!' she said, 'Your mom has a set of measuring spoons. Can't go wrong now. See, Bozo, it says "one tablespoon".'

'I can read,' I said coldly.

'Good, now put the water into the pan, put the heat on low and mix the cocoa in till it's a paste...' She came over as I switched on the gas, and watched, eagle-eyed.

'Okay, I'm going to semi-melt the butter in the microwave meanwhile...'

'The water seems too less; a lot of the cocoa powder is still dry...'

'Put in another spoon...'

The microwave beeped and she took out the shallow bowl of oozy butter and mixed it into the cocoa paste. What a mess!

'Okay, Bozo, give me that. You crack open the eggs in a bowl and add the sugar and start whisking it till it's light and frothy. You have a rotary beater, don't you?'

'I guess, must be somewhere... What does it look like?'

'This!' she said, showing me. 'Look at it carefully and memorize Bozo, so you can recognize it again anywhere!'

'Very funny!'

I whizzed the beater around; I had never realized that just sugar and eggs could be so stiff.

'Oh, we need to add a teaspoon of baking powder and pinch of salt to the flour. How's the mixing going, Bozo?'

'Great,' I said, whizzing away. Gradually, the sugar and egg mixture became lighter. 'This good?' I asked, lifting the beater out of the mix.

'Seems fine, great! Now we put the cocoa-butter mix into it. And now, add the flour bit by bit—but with a wooden spoon, and mix it in nicely... And lastly, we put in the walnuts.'

'Why wooden spoon?' I asked.

'Because that's what the recipe says, sweetheart!' she said sweetly.

I watched, fascinated by the colours—white, pale latte, dark brown, mixing in swirls. She glanced at me and grinned. 'Here, you mix it now, round and round, inside out, until it's all one delicious dark brown colour! It'll take a good fifteen minutes or so!'

'Man, you've got to be pretty organized for this cooking business,' I said.

'Yeah, someone once said that good cooks make good generals.' She grinned again, 'So watch out, Bozo!'

'I suppose that's why all the best chefs are guys!' I shot back, grinning.

'Excuse me? And this from someone who didn't know what a tablespoon was or what a rotary beater looked like! Right, now set the oven at 190 degrees Celsius.'

I looked blankly at the range and its various knobs. 'Um... which one is for the oven?'

'Ah, yes, General Chef...which is the oven knob...maybe we should try them one by one—we'll know when there's an explosion!' She pointed out a knob, 'This one! Commit to memory, Bozo!'

I looked at the dark chocolate-coloured mixture in the pan.

'No, don't you dare put a finger in to lick it. The flour is raw...but it is a bit like playing with mud, isn't it? Now we'll need a baking tray...'

'A what?'

'Ah, here it is…must say, your mom is pretty organized. Now we butter it…like this. Okay, now gently pour the brownie mix into the baking tray…easy does it!'

'Uh huh!' I looked at her. 'You know you really are one Miss Bossypants!'

'Thanks for the compliment!' She bent down and opened the oven. 'Ah, you've got an oven thermometer—good! Well it's almost 190, I think we can put the tray in.'

'How long will it take?'

'25 to 30 minutes. Now we better clean all this up. You know what detergent and a sponge is?'

'Haha! Show me!'

'Here, now get cracking! I'll be watching!'

The aroma that began wafting out of the kitchen in 20 minutes had my nose twitching.

'You know what's the worst part?' I said to her as we finished off with the cleaning. 'That we've made these brownies for the enemy!'

'As you keep saying, it's in the national interest. Of course, we're not going to give them the whole lot.'

The oven pinged after 25 minutes. 'Your mom must have oven gloves,' Chick said, opening the kitchen drawers one by one. 'Ah…yes, here they are…' She put them on and gently took the tray out. 'Watch out Bozo, it's very hot!' she warned as I hovered close. 'Keep your hands away!' She peered at the tray. 'They seem a bit too soft…' She plunged a sharp knife into them. 'Maybe a few minutes more…'

At last, she was satisfied that they were done. 'We'll let it cool and then cut them into squares.'

Of course you might think that Chick had taken charge of 'Operation Brownie' (so far), but I was the mastermind behind the bigger operation—if I hadn't spotted the terrorists arrive that night, none of this would have followed.

'They're okay,' Chick pronounced after we cut up the brownies, 'slightly chewy and moist, yet firm!' They were heavenly!

'They're yum!' I admitted, stuffing my face. 'Really great!'

She looked pleased. 'If you have some vanilla ice cream…' she said, standing beside me and rolling her eyes. 'We can go to heaven!'

Then, almost accidentally, our fingers brushed and just for an infinitesimal moment, tangled and interlocked before separating, as if they were doing something entirely of their own volition. We selected a dozen brownies for the enemy and put them on a tray. Just then, my phone rang. It was Aslam.

'Boss, the pigeons upstairs have flown downstairs! They're all together on the ground floor now! And when are you going to relieve me?'

'Okay, hang in there, we're on our way. We'll put 'Operation Brownie' into action!'

'Oh, wow! Bring some for me!' Before we disconnected, we heard the plaintive wails of his mouth organ. 'Oh shit,' I grinned, 'he's been playing his mouth organ!'

'Thank god, he's there by himself!' Chick said rolling her eyes again.

'Okay, guys so this is it!' I said as we made our way to the enemy camp yet again. Chick was carrying our 'token of friendship'. We'd eaten some brownies ourselves of course, with vanilla ice cream, which she had brought from her fridge.

We trooped up to the front door and Aslam rang the bell. We braced ourselves. Again, an eye appeared in the peephole and the door creaked open slowly. It was the tall ground floor terrorist who opened the door.

'Yes?' he inquired, 'Your ball has come into the garden again?'

'No…no, Uncle, we just made these brownies for you…to apologize for that!' Chick said, thrusting the tray under the guy's nose. He'd covered up his face just the way girls riding scooters often do. Only the mouth up to the bridge of the nose was uncovered. His eyes glittered out of the slits.

'Oh,' he looked taken aback. Then the brownies nailed him! Tentatively, he put out a hairy hand, picked one and put it into his mouth.

'Good!' he nodded, 'Very good! You made?'

'Yes, Uncle! They are walnut brownies. We…we'll bring the tray in…' Chick held on firmly to the tray.

'And Uncle, we're thirsty. Can we have some water, please?' Aslam asked.

I checked the fellow out. About six-feet tall, wearing a beige kurta and blue jeans, swarthy by the look of his arms, average build; couldn't make out his hair or the features of his face because of the black muffler-like thing wrapped around it. Kolapuri chappals. No bulges under his clothes that might conceal weapons, as far as I could tell, but kurtas are notoriously good for hiding that sort of thing.

For a moment, he looked nonplussed. Then, he nodded.

'*Achcha*, one moment.' He vanished into the dark hallway, leaving the door open. We heard him say something, and then, he was back at the door just as I was wondering if he'd gone to pick up his guns. 'Come in,' he said, opening the door as we trooped in. We entered the living room, still pretty dark because the curtains were drawn. The other three were sitting around the coffee table with the map of Mumbai spread open before them. Certain parts had been circled in red. Aslam nervously put the mouth organ to his lips and drew out a few hideous notes. Everyone looked at him.

The guy who had let us in yesterday was sitting next to the nervous-looking lady. The person next to her, in a purple tent-like garment, had quickly covered her head as we entered, but not before I saw she was female. She had a dark ponytail which she hastily knotted into a bun and tucked away at the nape of her neck before covering her head. So, we had two male and two female terrorists. And I knew it was always easier for females to enter high security areas than males; they probably weren't searched as thoroughly as men.

'These are...err...my friends,' the tall fellow mumbled as the others nodded and I assumed smiled wolfishly behind their masks. 'These children have made us these...brownies. They would like some water.' The nervous woman rose with a rustle of her clothes and waddled off towards the kitchen.

'It's very dark in here,' Chick said, 'why don't you draw the curtains?'

'Very hot here,' the tall man said, 'we like it dim...it's cool. Please sit!'

We sat awkwardly and Chick put the brownies on the coffee table, next to the map. I raked the map and took in my breath sharply.

The Gateway of India! The Prince of Wales Museum! A section of Marine Drive opposite the aquarium! The Hanging Gardens! Victoria Terminus or Chhatrapati Shivaji Station as it's now called! Worse: Some of the city's most famous places of worship and malls.

All encircled in red.

These guys were going for the kill in a big way.

'Err…you're here to sightsee?' Chick asked, her eyes flicking over the map. The nervous man nodded and quickly folded it up.

'Yes, we want to sightsee,' he mumbled.

'But…aren't you staying a little too far away… It takes at least two and a half hours to get into central Mumbai from here by road,' Chick said, sounding puzzled.

'Yes, it's very far,' the ground floor terrorist admitted. 'But very nice and quiet here.'

'We like the sea,' the woman who had covered her hair said. She had a quiet, husky voice. 'You would,' I thought sardonically, 'considering you came by boat.'

'How did you know about this place? About Dr Dubash?' Chick asked. I was glad we had brought her along; it's always more normal for chicks to ask such nosy questions.

'We read a blog on the net,' the nervous man said. 'And… some friends told us. Dr Dubash and his wife—very kind people.'

'Where are you from?' Chick asked, getting really chatty now. I think she'd forgotten how dangerous these people could be, that she had to be careful of what to ask, and how she asked them questions.

'From the north, Delhi side,' the tall man said as the woman returned with a tray and three stainless steel glasses.

'Thank you,' we said, helping ourselves. Don't know about the others, but my mouth had gone dry, and my palms were sweaty. There was a very good reason for that.

I had just spotted something that had made my blood run cold, and which I don't think the others had seen. Right next to the nervous fellow, thrust hastily under a pile of cushions at one end of the sofa, right beside the armrest, was the black butt of a gun, poking out. A gun butt—and the gun it belonged to, that I recognized only too well.

The last time I had seen it was in the hands of Dr D as he had put a tomcat with a broken back out of its misery, after a terrible fight with a rival. It had fluorescent orange sticker tape attached to the base of the butt; 'Like a warning triangle you put out when your car breaks down,' Dr D had told us.

The gun was just inches away from the nervous guy. He could whip it out and finish off all three of us in seconds. The Annex was isolated enough—no one would hear the shots. It was time to leave.

'It's so nice to have people staying here,' Chick said, fiddling with her plait and smiling. 'Usually, there's no one here but us.' She smiled brilliantly. 'Can we take our pictures with you?' she asked.

'Err...no, please, not now!' the husky voiced woman protested. 'You come again and we'll take picture.' She looked apologetically at her clothes. 'We're not dressed nicely!'

I shot Chick a warning glance and shook my head faintly. My eyes swivelled to the gun cushion. Got to say, Chick catches on fast; her eyes followed mine and widened just slightly.

'Uncle...h...how long are you staying here?' she managed to ask, her brilliant smile now very forced.

'Oh, a few days...' the man answered vaguely.

'And you'll be going back to...err...Delhi?'

He nodded and the others joined in.

'Very nice brownies!' the nervous woman said, picking one up.

'I can give you the recipe,' Chick offered generously. 'It's very easy. Even Bozo could make them! I'll bring the recipe next time we come!' She got up, her eyes still flicking towards the gun cushion. Aslam had taken no part in the conversation; but that was typical.

'Wait, I'll return the tray!' the nervous woman said, picking it up and going into the kitchen. She put the brownies on a plate and returned the tray to Chick.

'Thank you,' she said softly and placed her hand on Chick's.

'Whew! I think we escaped being shot by the skin of our teeth!' I said as we scrambled back up into the tree house.

'What the heck are you talking about?' Aslam asked.

'While you were sitting there dumbly in a trance, I kept my wits around me and looked about. Didn't you see it? Dr D's Smith and Wesson stuffed under the sofa cushion? The one he usually loads with blanks to scare off the monkeys except that time when he put that crippled tomcat down...'

'What?'

'Yes. Lambu spotted it too.'

Chick shook her head. 'I can't believe it,' she said. 'I just couldn't believe my eyes. And you're right—it is Dubash Uncle's gun! I remember the orange tape and him shooting that injured cat with it. He said he'd bought it on a trip to the US and has a license and all on account of where we live and that he loads it with blanks because there are so many kids around and accidents can happen.' She sounded shocked. She shook her head. 'What I don't understand is why he gave it to terrorists who are already heavily armed? It doesn't make sense!'

'Maybe...maybe, it's the smallest, easiest to carry weapon they have. All the others are probably AK-47s and...and rocket launchers and stuff like that—big and bulky...' It didn't sound very convincing but it would have to do for now.

'Man,' Aslam said, his eyes nearly popping out. 'And I missed it! If I had seen it I would have made a grab for it and held them hostage!'

'Like they are trembling schoolgirls or something!' I said sarcastically. Chick shot me a poisonous look. But she was still looking pretty dazed.

'You'd gone pretty pale in there, Bozo,' she said. Obviously, she was trying to project her own terror on to me. Hah! This was classical 'displacement'.

'I did see that they had marked all the important places in Mumbai,' Aslam said sheepishly.

'So, do we tell the cops now?' I asked.

'We still don't have concrete evidence—like pictures. We've only seen one gun, which they can easily hide, or return to Dr D if they sense trouble. As for the map, well, any tourist would want to see the places they've marked. So, what's so suspicious about that?' Chick shook her head. 'We've made discoveries but we've still not got any concrete evidence!'

'So, what now?' Aslam asked.

'Stake-out tomorrow. They'll have to go to Mumbai sooner or later. Tomorrow's Sunday. My guess is that they'll plant the bombs on Wednesday or Thursday. They're leaving on Friday, according to that ticket...'

'Maybe they did their recce before coming here,' Chick said. 'They might have been staying in Mumbai earlier.'

I nodded. 'That's possible. But let's stake-out anyway,' I said. 'If they do leave, it'll give us the chance we need to search the Annex and we can't miss that!'

'I guess,' Chick agreed reluctantly. 'They must be getting pretty fed up cooped up in the dark there all day.'

'We'll keep to the same routine we kept today,' I said. 'Lambu and I will take the 7 a.m. to 8.30 a.m. shift, then Aslam fills in till say 10, and we're back till 1.00 p.m. Aslam can do the afternoon shift. I think we could call it off by 4 p.m.—it'll be too late for them to leave for a recce then...'

We dispersed after that. At Bedlam House, Mridula Aunty's last session for the day had just gotten over. The dogs and their owners were getting into their cars and leaving. I went home. Man, it was weird entering a completely empty flat; it was just so quiet. No sound of anyone moving around, or Sohail whining, or kitchen utensils clattering, or even anyone breathing. Spending the night home alone was not going to be as much fun as I had imagined. Then, the doorbell rang. It was Chick.

'Hi! Mridula Aunty sent me up to keep you company,' she said. 'She said, "The poor boy is all alone." She's gone off to the village now to buy some fish and stuff. They have dinner at 8.30, so, we have to be back by then.'

'Oh, yeah, I was fine actually!'

'So should I go back?'

'No! Let's take a Frisbee to the beach and play with Night and Cactus, or let's show Aslam the hidden cove!'

'Okay.'

'I'll ring Aslam!'

We did both! We piled the dogs into The Bedlam along with Aslam, and purred off across the lagoon. We slowed down as we approached the northern end.

'Lambu, check for observers on the beach!' I ordered.

'Clear, Bozo, let's move!' I gunned the motor and before we knew it, we rounded the right hand bend and were out of sight of the beach.

'Man!' Aslam said his eyes wide. 'And to think we never guessed!'

We showed Aslam the way around the base of the tower. His eyes were goggling!

'Want to go up?' I asked. Chick glared at me, but I shook

my head faintly.

'Sure man, what are we waiting for?' Aslam exclaimed.

'You guys go!' Chick said, 'I'll stay here with the dogs. It's too risky for them.' I moved close to her.

'Don't worry, I won't unearth your friends,' I whispered.

She gave me one of her looks.

Aslam and I went up and returned in about twenty minutes. He was so zapped! Below, Chick was sitting on the rocks, looking as they would say, pensive, with her arms around the necks of both the dogs, and her long plait being gently tugged this way and that by the breeze. Then, we went back to the cove and had a great time playing Frisbee in the shallows there, getting completely soaked in the process. Night and Cushion went nuts. Cushion chased the huge Rottweiler all over the little beach, yapping away.

'Have you ever seen such a henpecked dog?' Chick said, dissolving into giggles.

'Cushy, come here, girl, let the poor guy be!'

Damp and sandy, we wrapped up by around seven and went back, making our way across the lagoon, now turning to pure gold in the sunset.

'Oh, someone's come,' I said, pointing to a white Innova in the car park. There were two guys in the lobby, tall well-built men with 'outdoor' faces—tanned and tough. They looked like rich farmers. One had a handlebar moustache; the other had a curly black beard and a gold earring. Both wore massive gold rings on their fingers and had fancy chunky wristwatches, with gold bracelets. They were both wearing long beige tunic-like kurtas and khaki jeans. They looked like brothers. And tugging away at leashes around their feet were two gorgeous German Shepherd pups, maybe two months old. The pups saw Night and quickly sat down side by side, their floppy ears down. Night gamboled up to them and they both turned turtle and surrendered. The Cactus, of course, started yapping.

'Don't worry, bhaisahib,' Chick assured them, indicating that I hold on to Night. In her arms now, Cactus was yapping away indignantly. 'He won't harm them. He's an idiot! But they're so sweet!'

'Training memsahib *kab ayega* (When will the training madam come)?' one of the men asked, raking all three of us with a piercing look.

'She'll be here any moment now,' Chick said, smiling. She was itching to pet the pups, but with Cactus in her arms, she had no chance. The pups had gotten over their fright and had begun playing with the Rottweiler.

'Class *kab hoata hain* (When do classes take place)? *Inko sikhana hain* (We want to train them),' he pointed at the pups, one of which had made a puddle.

'You'll have to ask madam,' Chick said, thrusting her plait behind her as Aslam started being goofy with the pups.

'Okay, we will wait!'

We went up to our respective flats to bathe and change.

Chick opened the door when I reported to the Dubashes for dinner at eight o' clock. She was barefoot and had changed into maroon capris and a pink top. I pretended not to notice how risky its neckline was when she leant forward. Her hair was tied in a long ponytail.

'Hi, come in!'

'I see you unravelled your rope,' I said, jerking my chin towards her ponytail.

'Uh huh. You can braid it again if you like!'

'As if!!' My eyes narrowed. 'Noticed anything suspicious?'

Her face closed up for a second. 'No. All normal here.' She frowned, 'I still can't believe it. Why would Dr D give his gun to those guys?'

'We'd better watch what we say. They shouldn't suspect that we know...'

'I can't believe they'd be involved in something like this.'

'It's okay, Lambu (I nearly called her "kiddo" but); we just have to swing with the punches!'

Dinner was fabulous tomato soup and delicious smoked fish with crisp finger chips, cream of spinach, baby carrots, and it finished off with leftover brownies and ice cream which Chick had insisted I bring down.

'Aunty, there were two guys with German Shepherd pups waiting for you this evening,' I said. 'Did they meet you?' She nodded.

'Yes, Nitu told me and I met them.' She smiled. 'They want me to train the pups in two weeks flat. They're rich farmers from upcountry—some remote village in Haryana or UP, where they have large farms and orchards...rather like we do. They came to Mumbai to acquire the pups and said they have to return home in a fortnight, so if I could train the pups in that time...' She shrugged prettily. 'The pups are so small!'

'Can they be trained so quickly?'

'Well, they are intelligent pups. I'll see how much they can pick up in that time and instruct those fellows...often you have to train the owners much more than the dogs...'

'They were lovely pups.'

Mridula Aunty sighed. 'Well, they're bringing the pups in tomorrow morning. And I'm starting an afternoon session too with the regulars. There goes my Sunday!'

Dr D was out on a house call and had rung to say he'd be late. He turned up at around 9, his usual booming cheerful self.

'Hello kids!' He lowered his voice to a conspiratorial whisper. 'How're the war wounds, eh?' he asked, his eyebrows shooting up.

'They're fine, Uncle,' Chick said, 'actually we'd forgotten about them! They've healed perfectly.'

'Good! Just don't go and do it all over again!'

At around 9.45, I got up to leave.

'*Beta*, are you sure you'll be all right, all by yourself upstairs?' Mridula Aunty asked me, looking worried. 'I told your mom you could spend the night here if you liked...'

I paused and glanced at Chick. She was looking at me. Was there mute appeal in those dark leopard's eyes? 'Please, please don't leave me alone here tonight... I'll be alone here with two potential killers or at least accomplices of killers...!' It was fine during the day, but at night...at night, I knew, all kinds of demons arose...

Of course I wasn't worried about myself, I was thinking about Chick...

5

'*U*m...' I frowned doubtfully. Of course *I* wasn't scared or anything like that, but there's something creepy about a silent, empty house at night; it tends to make all kinds of creaky and whispery sounds on its own which can freak you out. Mridula Aunty looked at me shrewdly.

'*Beta*, it can get very quiet in an empty flat at night,' she said. Hell man, the lady was reading my mind! I knew she meant 'and very scary too,' but she never said it. She's like that, you know.

'Yeah, Bozo, stay over; it'll be fun!'

'Um...okay...if it's not a hassle...' But of course! What was I thinking? As I just mentioned, Chick would be petrified staying here during the night, all on her own; as her superior (commanding officer), I couldn't ditch her like that.

'No problem at all, dear. I've given Nitu the guest bedroom so I'll put you in the second bedroom next to Uncle's study.'

'Aunty, if you take the sheets out I'll make his bed up for you,' Chick offered. 'While he goes up and fetches his toothbrush and pyjamas and teddy bear.'

I glared at her and she grinned back at me.

Half an hour later, I was ensconced in my room. Mridula Aunty popped her head around the door and said goodnight, bringing me a mug of cocoa and two digestive biscuits.

'You can watch TV as long as you like and wake up at whatever time you want, dear,' she said and smiled kindly. 'There's a TV in Uncle's study next door. But don't forget to brush your teeth after eating those biscuits. Goodnight dear!' And then, even I wondered how someone so sweet could be so mixed up in the evil plans of terrorists. If she had kids of her own, they would be spoilt rotten! I was wandering what Chick was up to, when there was a soft knock on the door.

'Hey, Bozo, are you awake?'

I let her in. She was in denim shorts and a loose white sleeveless top, several sizes too large for her.

'Hi...come in. Have they gone to bed?'

She nodded. 'Yes, Mridula Aunty brought me some cocoa and biscuits and said I could watch TV!'

'You have a TV in your room?'

'Yes!'

'Oh, well, let's go to the study! We can check it out.'

Dr D's study had wall-to-wall bookshelves. Not only heavy medical tomes, but also history, and a lot of biographies—Martin Luther King, Swami Vivekanada, Nehru, Einstein, Dr Christian Bernard (who did the first heart transplant), Lincoln, and a lot of other big guns. There were a lot of books on types of governments too—democracy, feudalism, tyranny, dictatorships and on sociology and anthropology and so on. He really seemed to be into heavy stuff. It seemed like Mridula Aunty also shared bookshelf space with him for there were a lot of doggie training books too and books about dogs in general. There were two desks, brown and gleaming, both neat. Medical papers and files piled up on one side, with a white coffee mug (depicting Angry Birds!) crammed with pens and pencils on Dr D's table and a blue pottery mug on Mridula Aunty's. There was an easy-boy lounger with a small table beside it, a Sony flat-screen TV and Bose music system placed against one wood-panelled wall. But no computer; neither desktop nor laptop. We were busy rummaging when Chick suddenly cocked her head.

'Footsteps! Just outside! Get under the desk on the double!' she hissed, pushing me down before I knew what was happening. I sat down and backed up against one side. She followed quickly and we were squashed shoulder to shoulder, barely daring to breathe.

We sat quiet as mice but there was no sound of the door opening and no one came in; it was a false alarm. 'Seems to be all clear,' she whispered in my ear, her lips soft against it. I nodded. She shifted sideways out and I followed. The straps of her loose top slipped down her shoulders as she scrambled to her feet and I looked at her and went hot and red.

'Ooops!' she squealed softly, and then, hissed, 'Bozo!' as I goggled at her. She drew up her top with as much dignity as she could manage.

'So...sorry!' I stuttered, completely scarlet and averting my eyes. 'I didn't...'

'It's cool, I know, you're fifteen!'

'They're so sweet, aren't they?' I said hastily, changing the subject, 'The Dubashes, I mean,' I added hastily, going even redder.

She smiled sardonically and straightened her top.

'Oh them, well, yes, of course...'

I shook my head darkly. 'It's a bad business, this,' I went on. 'The sooner we get to the bottom of it, the better!'

'Maybe we can,' she said and opened out her hand. She was holding a small memory stick. 'See what I found under the desk. It must have fallen and got kicked underneath.'

'Wow, let's check it out!'

We went to her room and she opened her laptop.

'I just hope this doesn't have some nasty and deadly virus that'll kill my laptop,' she said, looking at me. But she stuck it in. 'Fingers crossed!'

'Well?' I asked, 'Got anything?'

'Damn!' she said, 'it's password protected! Hmm...let me see...'

But we had no luck in opening any of the files, or anything at all. At length, she gave up.

'Let's sleep on it,' she said. 'Trouble is, I can't even copy it... otherwise we could have put it back after doing so.'

'Well, if it was under the desk, Mridula Aunty must have thought she had lost it, not that someone's taken it.'

'I guess.'

Chick swished her elephant's tail; it was loose again, and grinned. 'Okay, Bozo, now braid my hair again please, if you don't mind!'

'Why did you open it up again?' I grumbled. She grinned.

'So you could practise! See how much you've learned today! How to braid a girl's hair and how to make brownies. Any girlfriend will be over the moon with that, so you owe me, buster!'

'I don't have a girlfriend and don't intend to have one,' I said with great dignity.

'Sure,' she said laconically and leaned her head back against my chest again. 'Sure! Now let me lean my head against your manly chest for a bit...mmm!' This time, she let it rest there for a bit.

'Excuse me, what the heck do you mean by that?' I demanded, getting hot under the collar.

'Go figure, Bozo, go figure!' she snorted, looking up at me and giving me her witch's smile again. 'Now get cracking!'

I have to admit I wasn't quite looking forward to spending another day in the tree house, playing stake-out. It must have been worse for Aslam who did his stints alone. At least Chick and I were together and it's so much easier to pass the time with someone rather than alone. Well, Aslam did have his keyboard and mouth organ and he didn't seem to mind.

Still, we set forth at 6.45 a.m. the next morning, as usual. The Dubashes too had woken early. Mridula Aunty was expecting the guys with the German shepherd pups, and Dr D had to go to Mumbai for some work. Chick and I did our first morning stint and returned at around 9, having had to rouse a sleepy Aslam as usual. Out on the lower lawn, Mridula Aunty was with the two German shepherd pups and their owners—classes had begun! The pups were being taught to 'sit' and 'stay'. We watched. The session was brief because so was the pups' attention span.

Aunty and Uncle joined us for breakfast a little later.

'I hope you had a comfortable night, my dears,' Mridula Aunty said as Dr D emerged from the kitchen with a redolent and gigantic fluffy omelette in a pan.

'Fine, Aunty.'

'How was the training session?' I asked.

'The pups are smart, but they're still very small and get easily distracted. But the owners seem really keen to have them trained. They've asked to stay here and watch me take classes with the other dogs, so that they can do the same when they go back. They even asked if they could video me do that.'

'What did you say?'

'Oh, I have no problem. My sessions are already on YouTube, and there's nothing secretive about them. The more people there are who can train dogs, the better I think!'

She smiled wryly and looked at us. 'Kids, would you do me a favour, please?' she asked. We nodded. (What else could we do?)

'Um…those two gentlemen are going to be hanging around here all morning, waiting for the afternoon session. It doesn't make sense for them to drive all the way to Mumbai, where they're based, and back again; they said they haven't managed to get a place in the town as yet. So, I told them they could wait here—it'll be less tiring for the pups too. So, maybe you could show them around? They are also farmers and seemed quite keen to see the place... I would have normally asked Raman (the farm manager) to do so, but he's down with viral fever.'

'Sure Aunty, no problem!'

'They've gone to the dhaba in the village for breakfast and said they'd be back by around ten o'clock.'

'Okay, we'll check in before that and show them around.'

'Thank you dears. I have a house call to make in the morning—a spaniel suffering from acute separation anxiety. But I'll be back by lunchtime.'

'Oh crap, that's torn our stake-out timetable,' I told Chick as we made our way back to the tree house after breakfast, to relieve Aslam. Judging by the plaintive mouth organ notes emerging from the tree house, he wanted to be relieved—pronto!

'Well, maybe Aslam can do longer shifts,' Chick said. 'Personally, I'm not complaining. I have had enough of sitting around in the tree house doing nothing.'

'Sorry, no can do,' Aslam said, shaking his head when we told him. 'I have another music class this morning. Sir's getting pretty nervous! Mom says I have to go and she's taking me!'

Chick tossed her head. 'It's okay, we'll just split up then, I guess. One of us does the stake-out, the other shows those guys around. We'll toss!' We did. Damn! I had to do the stake-out while Chick showed the visitors around.

But that became unnecessary. Chick was just about to leave

the tree house at around 9.45 a.m., when she grabbed my hand.

'Bozo! Look!' she hissed and pointed.

Dr D was walking down the path towards the Annex, in his long grey shorts, a white bush-shirt and a straw hat. He went up to the front door of the ground floor and knocked. The door was opened, and he disappeared inside. A few minutes later, the couple living upstairs descended, looking furtively around. Both were in long tunic-like kurtas (the man in dark green, the woman in yellow) and had their heads and faces covered, gangster style. They disappeared into the ground floor unit. A few minutes later, they all came out. They shut and locked the front door and then, with Dr D in the lead, headed towards the playground. They would pass from virtually right under the tree house. Chick and I exchanged glances and ducked down.

'I've ordered a taxi to meet us at the Taj Hotel by around 11.30 a. m.,' Dr D said as they hurried by. 'He'll take you around wherever you wish to go. You can meet me at the Taj again by 7.00 p.m. and I'll bring you back here.' He glanced at his 'guests'. 'Don't miss Chowpatty beach at sunset though,' he said and laughed. 'Or the Queen's Necklace from Hanging Gardens! Those places are very crowded. You'll be all right there!' Yes, I thought, they certainly are the most crowded...

The men mumbled something, as they ushered the women along. The only saving grace was that they didn't seem to be carrying any heavy weapons. So, this was probably just a reconnaissance trip to check out potential targets. I moved up to Chick.

'We follow them,' I whispered into her ear.

The party left the playground and made their way past Lotus Lake and through the lower garden. We followed discreetly. They went down the rocky steps onto the beach and headed for the jetty at the southern end of the beach.

'Oh, he's taking them to Mumbai in The Lily of the West!' I said. From the garden itself, we watched the boat set off, nosing its way through the passage in the reef, until it was out in open water.

'Well!' Chick said, grinning, hands on her hips. 'That leaves us free to have a look at the Annex without interference!'

'You have to show those German shepherd guys around,' I reminded her, glancing at my watch. 'They should be here any minute now. I can go and check out the Annex!'

'No way, Bozo! I want to be there when we check it out. I'm not going to miss that for anything!'

'Okay, we have the whole day, no problem! We'll check out the Annex this afternoon. Those guys are not returning until after dark! I can help you show the German shepherd guys around too.'

'Okay, great!'

Have to say, those two German shepherd guys turned out to be pretty cool and savvy. They were punctual, carrying black shoulder bags, with the pups in tow. They smiled warmly when Mridula Aunty introduced us to them.

'Children, these are Shri Vivek and Ajit Thakur who have come all the way down from Hamirpur in Haryana.' She smiled at the guys. 'And these are Rohan and Nitu. They've grown up here and know every inch of the place like the back of their hands; they'll be happy to show you around. You can later sit in the waiting room and have tea and coffee if you like,' she said hospitably, as she bade us goodbye and got into her bronze Duster. 'The children will take care of you!'

'Hello,' we said together as they shook our hands. 'Hard hands, firm grip, not pleasant to have around your throat,' I thought wryly. Chick looked at the pups, who were gamboling around at our feet. 'What are their names?' she asked, smiling.

'Bobby and Tommy,' one of the men said. Chick winced and tried to hide her disappointment.

'They're beautiful dogs. Must be pedigreed,' I said.

'*Hanji*, foreign, imported *hain*...'

'You and your *bhenji* (sister) have lived here all your life?' Vivek asked us as we began a tour of the farm. I was about to correct him about the '*bhenji*' part, when Chick interrupted , with a sly grin and a nudge.

'*Hanji*, yes...we were born here. Actually, our parents are tenants of the Dubashes.'

'Dr Dubash and his good wife, very nice people... It is a beautiful farm, very well-kept.'

'She's a very good dog trainer. The dogs listen to her.'

'Yes,' Ajit agreed, 'already these fellows are listening to her. When she says *baitho*, they sit; but they don't listen to us!'

'Uncle, you can leave the bags in aunty's waiting room if you like,' Chick offered. The men shook their heads. 'No, it is fine, no problem.'

Most people didn't like leaving their bags in strange places. 'Not unless they contained explosives, timed to go off,' I thought grimly, thinking of the eight suitcases and four rucksacks in the Annex.

We took the Thakur fellows around the chickoo and mango orchards, the coconut groves, the paddy fields, the vegetable gardens, the playground and Lotus Lake, but of course, did not show them the tree house. That was on a strictly 'need-to-know' basis, and they didn't need to know. Both Night and Cactus accompanied us, much to the delight of the pups.

'What's that?' one of the men asked, pointing to the Annex. 'Does somebody live there?'

'Oh that's sort of a retreat or holiday home that the Dubashes give out on rent,' Chick explained.

'Oh...can we have a look, please? Maybe we can come here for a little holiday. It's very peaceful...with cool sea breeze and trees and birds.'

'Someone's rented it for now,' I said, 'in fact, both floors. They've gone out at the moment.'

'Usually people don't stay very long, so you could ask Mrs Dubash if they will be vacant after these people leave,' Chick offered helpfully.

'Thank you *beti*, we will.'

'How many rooms?' the other man asked.

'Two bedrooms in each, a living and dining room verandah as you can see, a small hallway, two bathrooms and a kitchenette,' Chick rattled off as if she was selling the place.

'And you get a view of the sea from the verandahs,' I added. 'Let's see if we can peep inside.' I led the way into the garden and we tried peering through the French windows in the verandahs. Of course, the heavy curtains had been drawn. But there are always slits between curtains; somehow they never quite manage to meet properly in the middle. We cupped our hands and peered through them.

'You can get an idea of the living room,' I said, backing away and making way for one of the guys. I glanced at the front door and my heart sank. There was a huge brass padlock locking the deadbolt; if we wanted to go in and search, we'd have to break and enter in a big way. I had no doubt that the front door to the first floor would be similarly locked; as also the outside bathroom doors. Damn!

Both men peered through the crack sheepishly. Then, one of the pups wriggled his way beneath one of the cane chairs in the verandah, and emerged with something fluttery and white in his mouth. It was a ladies' handkerchief!

'Hey, give me that!' Chick said, 'Leave it! You can't eat that!' She managed to take the handkerchief from the pup before a tug-of-war could ensue with its sibling and Cactus.

'Just look at it,' she suddenly exclaimed. 'It's got such beautiful intricate embroidery on it... Actually, it looks like calligraphy!' Well, chicks would go for that sort of thing, but I barely glanced at it, as did the two fellows. Then, one of them suddenly stiffened and glanced at it again.

'*Beti*, can I see that, please?' His piercing eyes raked the scrappy piece of material and he handed to his friend, muttering something low under his breath. Then, he smiled at us.

'Yes, very intricate design!' he said, 'Done by hand; very beautiful.' I was a bit surprised: the fellow's face had gone red, and his nostrils were flared.

'It must belong to one of the ladies,' Chick said, as the men handed her back the handkerchief. 'We'll give it back to them when they return.'

'Err...how many people are staying now?' one of the men asked as we walked back through the lower garden.

'Four. Two couples actually,' Chick said, smiling. 'Very secretive really—they keep their faces covered at all times!'

'They had their own vehicle?'

'Umm...no, Dr Dubash brought them over by boat.' I said. 'Ah!'

'Would you like to go down to the beach now?' Chick offered. 'The pups can run around there nicely.'

'Okay, sure no problem.'

'Do you know how many days they're staying here for? Just so we can maybe do bookings for afterwards... Call our families over too. Then we can have a holiday here and the pups can be trained tip-top.'

'They're probably here till next Saturday,' I said. 'They're going abroad after that.'

'Foreign?' Both the men asked simultaneously. They exchanged glances. 'Um...does Mrs Dubash keep a guest register?' one of them asked.

'I guess, she does,' Lambu shrugged. 'Why?'

'Then she must have ID proof of them... That is mandatory.'

Whoa! Easy there, not so fast! Why the heck were these guys suddenly so interested in the Annex guests? My antenna began twitching. Chick didn't seem to suspect anything.

'I guess,' she went on, 'aunty's very particular about those kinds of things.'

'Why? Is something wrong? Do you know them?' I asked flat out. That's me—head-on interrogation, no pussy-footed tiptoeing around. I do the bad cop part well.

The men exchanged glances. Then, the taller of the two, Vivek Thakur, nodded faintly.

'Children...how to put it....this could be a matter of...of grave danger and...high national security...'

'What?' Both Chick and I stopped and gaped at them. 'How do you know that? How did you know they are terrorists?' I blurted.

'We are from SSIS: Super Special Intelligence Service... There...there was information that four suspected and very dangerous terrorists are holed up together not far from Mumbai—two men and two women.'

'But wait,' the other man said, staring at us, alarmed. 'How did *you* also know they were terrorists?'

'Bec...sir, because they arrived by boat in the middle of the night and were carrying heavy bags and are always covered up from head to toe!' It was on the tip of my tongue to tell him that we'd seen Dr D's Smith and Wesson in their flat, but I just couldn't do it. It would be like betraying him...even though he (and Mridula Aunty of all people!) had been betraying the whole country, royally. Suddenly, I banged my fist into my hand. 'Here, wait, I have a photo of one of them; and the passport the fellow is using...' I took out my phone and showed him the pictures Aslam had taken (and forwarded to me). The men peered at them and nodded slowly.

'That's the fellow, all right: he's the ringleader. They're members of the dreaded Katliyam Jihadi Mujahadeen...the KJM,' he went on.

'You know, I think they're planning to hit Mumbai,' I said excitedly. 'We saw a map of Mumbai with all the tourist places circled in red in their place.'

'Do you know when they are returning?'

'Tonight. Probably by around 9 p.m.'

'Ah!'

'Are the Dubashes mixed up in this?' I asked, not really wanting to know the answer. And suddenly, Chick was holding my hand and squeezing it hard. She, poor kid, was dreading the answer too. The taller man nodded slowly, regretfully.

'It seems so,' he said heavily. 'For long, they have been suspected of harbouring such people, but there was no proof.'

'So what are you going to do now?' Chick asked heavily. She had taken a solid blow. So had I. We had suspected, but now there was proof. And that damn Smith and Wesson under that cushion. That just about nailed the case against the Dubashes.

The taller 'Thakur' fellow looked at us. 'Have you told anyone about your suspicions?'

I grimaced. 'No. Who the heck do you think would have believed us? We're kids! They would have laughed!'

He nodded. 'Very sensible of you! Please tell no one at all. This is top secret—confidential.'

'Sure. No problem.'

The man smiled and lightly patted my back.

'Very good! Now please excuse us, we have to discuss this amongst ourselves,' he said. 'Here, play with the puppies for some time. We'll call you.'

We moved away and tried playing with the pups, but our hearts weren't in it. Everything was suddenly coming to the boil.

'I always knew there was something odd about those guys,' I told Chick. 'The way they turned up and said they wanted to hang around. They could have spent the morning in the fishing village or the town looking for a place, not here. Lucky for them, the terrorists have gone to Mumbai, otherwise who knows what would have happened.'

'Bozo, but what's going to happen now? They'll arrest Dr D and Mridula Aunty, won't they? And shoot up the terrorists... We'd better ring our parents...' There were tears in Chick's eyes.

'Are you nuts? They won't believe a word and think we've been watching too much rubbish video and make us join all kinds of idiotic summer classes! Poor Aslam is already in for it with his music... Besides, these fellows just told us to keep quiet about it.'

'So, we say nothing and just sit tight?'

'Yeah! We'll see what these guys plan. They'll have to take down the terrorists.'

The two men walked up to us after ten minutes.

'*Bachche*, listen carefully now,' Vivek Thakur told us. 'We're going to do this very quietly. We are required to take the terrorists alive. When they get back, we will just surround their building and knock them out with stun grenades. Another team will quietly take Dr Dubash and his wife into custody. No blood, no shooting, nobody gets hurt, nothing. We need to interrogate those terrorists and the doctor sahib and madam properly… We will of course have to inform your parents afterwards… So for now, you will continue to behave as if nothing has changed and nothing has happened. All right?'

Chick and I exchanged glances.

'Okay,' I said and shrugged. 'That sounds good.'

Vivek looked at his watch and smiled. 'All right, now we'll go to the village and have lunch and come back for the training class.'

'Um…sir; at the moment, both of us are staying with Dr Dubash and his wife in their flat,' Chick said. 'Our parents are out of station.' Good thinking, Chick! We certainly didn't want to get caught in any crossfire during a raid or something.

The tall man frowned. 'I see. Good you have told us that. We will tell you at what time we shall be coming to arrest them; you will have to make sure you are not in the flat then because there is always the chance that they might take you hostage. You can say you want to go for a walk or whatever, and leave the house. But we will inform you before we come.'

In a way, it was a relief, I guess. Neither I, nor Chick, wanted to be around to see the Dubashes being taken down. 'Tonight,' I thought grimly, 'there was going to be a lot of bedlam in Bedlam House.' And neither Chick nor I were looking forward to it.

6

$\mathcal{J}$ don't think either Chick or I enjoyed our lunch very much that afternoon. The SSIS guys had gone to the village for lunch and said they'd return to observe the afternoon training session. To our surprise, they asked if they could leave the puppies with us.

'Can you please look after them for now? We have to make plans and coordinate things. It is difficult with these two running around...'

'Sure!' Chick said, 'No problem.' She picked up one of the pups and kissed it. But I knew her heart was heavy.

'I just can't believe it,' she said for the umpteenth time. 'They've been like foster parents to us. How can they be involved in such things?'

'Well, you saw the gun too,' I said stoically. I was hurting too... But more from a sense of betrayal. 'Any luck with the memory stick?'

She shook her head.

'No, but I'll keep trying. Something will click sooner or later. Bozo, what will happen afterwards?' Chick asked, her hand creeping into mine. Poor kid, she was hurting bad. I squeezed her hand back.

'Dunno, chicklet,' I murmured.

And man, I knew she was real upset because she let it pass.

'We just have to be strong, I guess.' I patted her back reassuringly. 'Take it on the chin!' She looked at me, a strange glint in her eyes. Suddenly, she wrapped her long arms around me and hugged me real hard. Then, she let me go. Neither of us said anything. Got to admit (never to her), it felt comforting. A hideous thought—had I needed that hug too?

The SSIS guys returned in the afternoon to 'observe' the class—to keep up the subterfuge of course. We took the puppies to them and stood beside them, watching as the class got under way.

'It's been arranged,' Vivek, who was obviously the boss, softly told us. 'We've got teams in place, watching. When they spot the boat coming back with the terrorists, they'll move in. We'll wait till they've settled down and are sleeping in the house and then surround it. You will be informed by phone so you can get out of the flat of the landlords. Then we will arrest them. Should not be much of a problem, but you never know. We don't know what kind of arms or explosives they might be carrying.'

My phone rang. It was Aslam.

'Listen, mom's grounded me!' he said grumpily. 'She just wants me to concentrate on my music till the exam. No fooling around. She keeps saying I might cut my fingers or do something silly. I can't come for any more stake-outs till the exam's over.' I knew that disobeying her could be hazardous to his health. We hadn't even told him of the developments since that morning about what the farmers' real identity was and what had been planned for the night.

'Never mind, we'll keep you in the loop! Listen, I can't tell you any details, but stuff might happen tonight—serious stuff. Just look sharp and lay low, okay?'

'What?' he nearly freaked out. 'What kind of stuff?'

'Action downstairs!' I said succinctly, 'I'm under oath not to reveal any more. Got to go now, buddy.'

'It's not surprising his mom has put him under curfew,' Chick said when I told her. 'He'll get a fabulous scholarship if he tops that exam and that's what aunty's banking on. So he better be good and listen to her!'

'Poor guy, he's missing out big time, isn't he?' She looked at me strangely. I knew why—we wouldn't have minded missing out on something like this. It was not going to be a pleasant night.

We messed around in the evening, walking on the beach, with the puppies and Cushion and Night. Cushion seemed to be quite happy when Chick dropped her at Aslam's place afterwards (We couldn't have her with us that night when we snuck off; she would inevitably bark and rouse the household). Aslam loved her; he said she sat down on the piano stool beside him and listened as he played, cocking her head from one side to another. 'She's a classy little dog!' he grinned, 'Even mama is impressed!' That pleased Chick no end, but she didn't look very happy for long.

'I feel like that there's this great big boulder in my tummy,' she said. 'Like a major exam I have to take, about which I know nothing.'

I nodded briefly. I knew exactly what she meant.

'So...how do we get out when the call comes?' I asked. 'I guess I'll be spending tonight at the Dubashes again.'

She smiled wryly. 'Our usual way—down the madhumalti and drainpipe! I just hope we're not caught.'

'Dr D will have something to rag us about if they do catch us,' I said, which really was silly considering what was going to happen to them. 'We'll play it by ear,' I went on vaguely, nodding. 'Maybe we can just tell them we're going for a walk on the beach. He can do as much woo-woo he wants!'

'I really hate this!'

Then I got my brainwave. 'You know what we can do? We'll go to the tree house and watch the Anti-Terror Squad or SSIS or whatever take down the terrorists. We'd have a ringside view and neither they nor the terrorists know of the tree house.'

Chick looked at me sadly. 'Yes, I guess we could. At least it'll be better than seeing aunty and Uncle being taken into custody.'

Then, a very strange thing happened. I looked at Chick and found she was staring back at me. I think we both got the same idea at exactly the same moment.

'You know...' I started levelly. 'Dr D and Mridula Aunty have really been like parents to us...even if they do rag us a lot...'

'I think they've done more for us than our real parents,' Chick declared flatly.

'So we owe them...too...' I went on, sotto voce. 'We have to be loyal to them too... They....they deserve a second chance...'

Chick's eyes widened and her forehead creased. 'Bozo, are... you thinking what I'm thinking? That we...'

I gulped. It might seem like we were betraying the country, but everyone deserved a second chance. And we...I...owed them too for all they had done for us.

'We send them an anonymous e-mail, warning them to get out and never try this sort of thing again...' I told Chick.

Chick just stared at me as though I were crazy, her eyes glistening. Then, she came up to me and put her hand on my head and gently rubbed it.

'God, it's like petting a hedgehog!' she murmured and then she took me into her arms and hugged me tightly for the second time that morning.

'Bozo, how did you know I was thinking the same thing?' she asked huskily, taking my face in her hands and looking at me gravely. She drew back. 'I thought you'd never agree... I was thinking of doing this by myself...' Her eyes were shining with tears now. They looked like pearls.

'You were?'

She grimaced. 'Well, yes, what did you expect? You were full of your "eureka" gung-ho, perfect cover, let's nail 'em macho stuff!'

'I know… But it was all right just *imagining* things like that…it became different after those guys turned up, and when we found the gun… Now it's reality and…and…it's a bit hard to take.' I swallowed. She looked at me, her leopard's eyes inches from my face. Then she kissed me softly and drew back.

'That must've been tough for a tough guy like you to say,' she said, her voice husky and gentle.

'Lambu!' I gulped and swallowed. Was Chick trying to turn me into a marshmallow? I was kinda feeling that way… Okay, enough of this, time for cold, rational thinking. I got a hold of myself again.

'So, let's get this straight. We stay here as usual and wait for the SSIS to ring us… Then, we take off for the tree house…' I frowned. There was a flaw. If we did wait till the SSIS rang us, it would be too late to warn the Dubashes to make tracks; they'd need a little time to make a clean getaway. Chick spotted it at once.

'I don't think we should wait,' she said frowning. 'I think we should clear out as soon as the coast is clear. Once Uncle and aunty go to bed, we leave. We get to the tree house and send them the e-mail warning.'

'What if Night starts barking?'

We both smiled wryly. 'Nah, he won't! He sleeps with Uncle and aunty in their air-conditioned bedroom and doesn't stir until 9 a.m.!'

'You know, we'll be betraying the country by warning them…' I said with heavy drama. 'What if they escape and begin doing this kind of thing elsewhere? We might be responsible for the deaths of innocent people…' It sucked. The whole thing sucked.

Chick shook her head. 'I still don't believe they'd do something like this! It's like a bad dream. I wish we could wake up again and everything would be normal.'

I knew what she meant. I felt it in my bones as well. But the facts—that wretched gun, the SSIS fellows—spoke for themselves and told a different story.

'It just shows,' I went on heavily, 'you just can't trust anyone these days!'

At the time, I had no idea how right I was.

We were back at the Dubashes at 7.30 p.m. We quickly had our baths and changed into shorts and T-shirts—our usual nightwear. Then we hung out on the verandah, looking out at the sea. We were waiting for The Lily of the West to return. Mridula Aunty was in the study, working on her laptop. We both felt pretty lousy. This was a nasty business all right. At 8.00 p.m., Mridula Aunty joined us on the verandah.

'Kids, dinner will be a little late tonight,' she said. 'Uncle just called—he'll be back around 8.30, so we'll eat at 9.'

'Fine, Aunty, no problem.'

She went back into the study. At 8.40, we saw The Lily of the West nose her way through the reef entrance to the lagoon. She disappeared as she headed towards the jetty. The first floor of Bedlam House was too low for us to see the docking area at the base of the cliff and how many people were on board, unlike our flats upstairs. But we just had to wait. They would appear at the garden gate. They did—Dr D and his four terrorist 'guests'. All wrapped up as usual. They snuck their way towards the playground and Annex as Dr D headed home. Night ran out and met him, barking happily. We withdrew and shook our heads.

It was a bad business—a very bad and sad business indeed.

Our troubling thoughts obviously showed on our faces. At dinner that night—a redolent mutton biryani (talk about the last supper!)—Dr D eyed us both keenly and raised his eyebrows.

'You kids feeling all right?' he asked. 'Not as if you're coming down with something? You're looking a bit peaky and pale, both of you.'

'We're fine, Uncle, thanks.'

'Those cuts and nicks you collected—not bothering you?'

'No, they're fine.'

He nodded, came around and felt our foreheads.

'Hmm... No trouble in paradise between the two of you or anything like that?' he asked kindly and then winked, an affectionate smile crinkling his face.

'Dear, don't tease them,' Mridula Aunty admonished him.

'No, Uncle, everything's fine, really,' Chick said. 'Bozo has been as irritating as he usually is.'

'We're good!' I said hoarsely, 'really good!'

'Hmm...glad to hear that son, very glad to hear that!' He pursed his lips and his eyes crinkled with laughter. 'You two...so wonderful to see...' He smiled again, and began humming those words from that song '...to live, love...when the flame is strong...'

'Darling!' Mridula Aunty shushed him, taking his hand. 'Don't embarrass them!'

'They're our god kids! I have the right to embarrass them!'

'Don't listen to what Uncle says. You know, he loves teasing both of you.'

We put our heads down and ate our biryani, without really tasting it. To think we had ratted on them and would be deserting their sinking ship tonight. But at least we'd be throwing them a lifeline too—and letting down the country. We were betraying everyone!

'I feel just awful!' Chick said as she came into my room after dinner, 'Like we're doing that Judas thing to them by keeping quiet and not warning them. Maybe we should just tell them!'

I shook my head. 'No…it'll be better that we're nowhere around. They might just take us hostage, if they're really involved and all…'

I grinned wryly. It seemed such a ludicrous idea—being taken hostage by Dr D and Mridula Aunty.

'Yeah!' Chick said sardonically, 'I can just see Dr D hold his Magnum syringe at our jugulars, filled with cobra venom!'

We both grinned. But we had seen his Smith and Wesson in the terrorists' lair. There was no getting away from that. 'We both saw the gun,' I said heavily. 'That kind of puts the seal on it, doesn't it? They're in it up to their ears!'

'I guess.'

'You got everything you need?'

'Yes—rucksack, my laptop and the rest of the stuff. SOP.'

'Good! We'll sneak out by 1100 hours. They should be asleep by then.'

At 1105 hours, we were outside Bedlam House, keeping a lookout for the night watchmen. We snuck into the lower garden and, ducking low, made for the playground. Once, we just stopped and looked back at the grand yellow building that had been our home all our lives. It would still be there in the morning, but everything would be upside down—Dr D and Mridula Aunty would either have loaded up their Safari or taken The Lily of the West and fled, or be in the hands of the SSIS. Our whole world would have come tumbling down around our ears. What would our parents do? Would we continue living here? We hadn't the faintest idea.

'Just look at that moon,' Chick suddenly said. 'It's butter gold and just rising. And it's so full!' She sounded sad. 'It's so awful that such a terrible thing is going to happen on such a beautiful night.'

We climbed into the tree house, flashing our torches at the floor to check for creepy crawlies. The Annex was in darkness.

'Don't shine the torch at the windows,' I warned. Chick just gave me one of her looks. She settled down in a corner and opened her laptop.

'Okay, I'm going to send them the warning e-mail...' she said. 'I'll have to generate a new e-mail identity and password.'

'What identity?'

'Well-wisher,' she said. 'And I'm mentioning your e-mail ID as reference.'

'And password?'

Chick looked at me a little sadly. 'How about, 'Tolivelovewhentheflameisstrong?'

'That's very long.'

'But we'll never forget it.'

We sent out the first and probably last e-mail from the e-mail ID.

Dr Dubash and Ms. Mridula Dubash,
The SSIS are coming for you tonight.
From,
Well-wishers.

'We won't write anything about the terrorists in the Annex,' I said. 'They deserve to be taken down!'

'I guess. Okay, here goes!' She clicked the 'Send' button. 'It's done!' I hooded my eyes and nodded, trying to block out the turmoil in my head.

'Okay, I'll keep watch on the Annex, now. You rest,' I said briefly, as she shut her laptop. She glared at me and opened it up again—just like her.

An hour passed and nothing happened. I found myself nodding as I stared at the dark bulk of the Annex. Sometimes, a light would come on and then go off again. Chick just worked steadily on her computer.

'What are you doing?' I asked at last, 'You've been at your laptop for ages.'

'Hacking!' she said sarcastically.

'Oh, yes. Well, if it's a game, I'd like to join if I can.'

'Sure, Bozo, I'd let you know!'

'Any luck with opening the files on the memory stick?'

'No,' she grunted.

I glanced at her. Dappled by the moon pouring in through the wide slats in the tree house roof, she looked like some exotic, ethereal alien. Some would say, beautiful.

'It's past midnight and those SSIS guys haven't gotten in touch. I wonder when they're coming!' I yawned. 'They should have given us their number—we could have contacted them!'

I took out my iPod and plugged into some music—anything to keep one awake. It was going to be a very long night.

Stake-outs are like that—very, very long and dreary periods when absolutely nothing happens. And then suddenly action, action, action and all hell breaks loose!

And at around 3.15 a.m., the action began.

Chick was still hunched over her laptop, half-asleep. I still had no idea what she was doing.

'Any luck with the memory stick?' I asked again. She just shook her head and kept shutting it when I tried peering over her shoulder, so I got the message. Hacking, my foot! She must have been chatting with some obnoxious boyfriend—none of my business. I was almost dozing, and trying to stay awake by alternately staring at the Annex and then the sea. The sea was all silver and blue-black, the pale, peppermint creamers rushing up onto the reef to shatter, like frosted glass, luminous in the light of the moon. Then, suddenly, there was a dark bulk heaving on the waves—a boat! I peered through my bins. It was just beyond the reef but heading towards it—not The Lily of the West this time.

'There's a boat beyond the reef, trying to enter the lagoon now,' I muttered as Chick looked up from her laptop. 'It looks like a fishing boat from the village.' I glanced at her. 'Lambu, maybe this is it! The SSIS!'

'We haven't got a call,' she pointed out, coming to my side. 'Let me see!' Without bothering to take the strap off my neck, I handed her the bins. Our heads and cheeks bumped together as she peered through them.

'They're negotiating the reef,' she said softly. 'Quite well too; whoever's steering the boat knows the way in.'

The boat entered the lagoon. Now I could see the bulky silhouettes of five men, standing at the bow, looking towards the jetty. They all looked like they were carrying weapons of some kind—spears, swords and heavy sticks. Two men sat at the rear, near the engine; steering the boat, I guessed. But it was odd; they were not in camouflage or combat uniform or bulletproof jackets or carrying automatic weapons and RPGs. They didn't look like an anti-terrorist SWAT hit-team.

The moonlight was bright enough however, to reveal the identity of two of the five men—Vivek and Ajit Thakur. So, I guess they were SSIS guys after all, in mufti, perhaps to allay suspicion.

'It's them!' I said 'The SSIS team is here!'

'I just hope Uncle and Aunty have gone! There's been no reply to the mail!'

The quiet of the night was suddenly shattered by a sharp retort, like a shot and then a low rumbling noise, coming from the dark bulk of the Annex. We whirled around and stared at it.

The sliding doors on the first floor verandah of the Annex had been opened. The couple living there emerged on the verandah and stared up at the full moon—now, bright mercury silver and riding high in the night sky. I did a double take. The fellow was in a white kurta and jeans, the woman—get this—in jeans and a red halter! They embraced tightly and kissed.

Also, both their faces were uncovered. The man had a round plump face and was clean-shaven but for a neat goatee, and the woman, well, a young woman, I suppose, she was very fair and pretty, with big eyes and a snub nose. They looked like college freshers—not hardened terrorists. But then, terrorists had been training 10-year-olds for suicide missions, so what was so great about that? And college students were notoriously violent, everyone knew that. They loved throwing stones and setting fire to things at the slightest pretext.

Chick grabbed the bins from me and focused them on the couple.

'One of your mushy romances is coming true!' I grinned, 'But it's going to end in tragedy! Like Romeo and Juliet!'

She glared at me. 'Shut up, Bozo! It's not funny!'

The couple was really getting into a clinch now. 'Look at them!' I muttered, fascinated, appalled and a bit ashamed at the same time to be spying on them like this. I rolled my eyes and snorted. 'Talk about when the flame is strong!'

Chick gave me a startled look and glanced at the couple. Then, she darted to her laptop and furiously began typing.

'What are you doing?'

Her face was a study. She looked up at me and impatiently pushed her plait behind her.

'Bozo...' she said hoarsely, 'Bozo, come here and look at this!'

I peered over her shoulder. The website that had unfolded was called 'rescueromance.com' or something like that. Together, we read what was on the home page, and then clicked on one, titled, 'Rogue's Gallery'. A whole panel of pictures emerged—of couples—with their names, ages, and CVs.

Chick looked at me strangely. 'We were right and wrong,' she said huskily. 'This is Mridula Aunty's NGO's secret website. They help couples in love who are in trouble with their families to escape. Couples who are in danger of being victims of honour killing and worse! *That's* what they've been using the Annex for—as a sanctuary. They hide them here before they send them off abroad or elsewhere, where their families can't get them. See, here's the two...and the name is the same as in the passport!'

'How...how did you find this?' I muttered.

'I told you I was hacking! I needed one last password, and then you said it, in fact it's the same one we chose—'whentheflameisstrong'! Dr D must've driven Aunty nuts by humming that song all the time!' She looked stunned.

'So...so, who are the SSIS guys? I mean, they're on their way!'

Chick gave me a look. 'Angry and very nasty family members, I suppose,' she said. 'Remember how they reacted when they saw that handkerchief? My guess is that they recognized whose it was and then knew for sure that the people they were after were here. Remember how their attitude changed right after that?'

'So…so, they're here to take these guys back…'

'Against their will…I would imagine.'

'But they had all those weapons…'

'They're going to hurt them or kill them!' Chick whispered, horror-struck. 'And thanks to us, they know exactly where to find them.'

'But…what about the gun?' I asked.

'I don't know! Dr D must've given them that for self-defence or something. Come on, we have to warn them. And we'd better ring Dr D and Mridula Aunty right now and tell them too!'

As it always happens in crisis moments, we just couldn't get through to either Dr D or Mridula Aunty. Either their phones had been 'switched off' or were 'unreachable.'

'I'll try Aslam!' I said. The bell rang and rang, but he didn't answer it. 'Damn, he sleeps like the dead!'

'Or his mom has confiscated his phone and locked it away. Come on, we'll keep trying. Anyway, I think those guys will come here first before going to the house. They'll want to get their hands on these poor people first!' They were still in a clinch on the verandah. They'd been properly smitten by the moon.

'Let's go, let's go!'

We clambered down the rope ladder.

'Listen…' I said suddenly. I was just about to suggest that Chick go off to warn the Dubashes while I warned the couples in the Annex, when I realized that she might run straight into the so-called SSIS who would be heading this way. And if she warned the couples and I went off to warn the Dubashes, she might run into them again, before I returned with backup because the Annex would be their first priority. Either way, I could not have that happen under my command.

'What?' she snapped.

'Nothing, Chick, let's go!'

We heard the Annex doors rumble close again. The lovebirds upstairs had gone in.

'Lambu, you go ahead, I'll join you. I just want to see if those guys are coming...' I pushed her on and veered off towards Lotus Lake, keeping low. Chick made an impatient noise and charged off towards the Annex. I was soon hot on her heels. The so-called SSIS gang, now masked and with black bandanas on their heads, was striding swiftly up the lower garden towards the playground, led by Vivek and Ajit Thakur. They did not have friendly expressions on their faces. They looked ugly and grim.

'I'll go upstairs, you wake the guys downstairs!' Chick said, taking to the stairs two at a time.

I hammered on the front door and leant on the bell when I heard Chick do the same upstairs.

'*Kholo, kholo*! Open!' I shouted. 'Quickly!'

There was the sound of panicky voices inside and feet rushing about. Then, the door, still on the chain, opened and the ground floor man peered out, his eyes like a frightened rabbit's.

'*Kya* (What)?'

I glanced at his hands: Empty. I had been sure he'd be holding the gun, ready to fire. The fool was unarmed; maybe he'd just panicked and opened the door.

'Your family...father? Brother? Her father? Brother? Goondas? They're coming! Six men!' I stuttered inadequately. '*Hathiyaar leke*...with weapons!'

His face paled. And then Chick was downstairs, ushering in the two lovebirds we had just seen. Evidently, she'd been more persuasive than I had. The man downstairs saw them and opened the door and all of us piled inside. The tall downstairs guy was in shorts and a vest; he had curly hair and dark eyes and a mole on his chin. His wife or girlfriend or whatever—also very beautiful, but pale, and with hair rather like Chick's—was in a salwar kameez. She looked a lot like the girl upstairs.

'Hurry up, put on your shoes and we're out of here!' I yelled.

But we were already too late. We could hear footsteps scrunching outside on the gravel driveway. Someone pounded on the door with a fist. More feet thundered up the wooden steps to the first floor.

Chick looked at me desperately. 'Bozo, keep them distracted, I'll send these guys out through the bathroom door!' she said. I went near the front door, very nervously.

'*Kaun?* Who's there?' I asked. '*Kaun hain?*'

A stream of profanity came through the door. I blanched.

'*Aap ko kya chahiye jee* (What do you want please)?' I asked as politely as I could, almost trembling. '*Der raat hain* (It's late at night)!'

Another stream of profanity and now they were putting their shoulders to the door.

'*Abbe, kholta ki nahin* (Are you going to open or not)?'

'*Aap ko kuchch bechna hain kya* (Have you come to sell something)?' I asked, feeling like a complete moron and wanting to run like mad. These guys would flay me alive if they caught me. But it did distract them. It drove them to distraction actually.

I got another load of profanity. They were losing it.

I backed away and glanced over my shoulder. Chick was still in the bedroom.

'*Jao!* Go!' I heard her urge our refugees, through all the hammering. She was desperately pushing the petrified foursome into the bathroom. There was an outside door, from which, they could escape. Suddenly, she was back at my side in the hallway, grabbing my arm.

'Why didn't you go with them?' I asked appalled. The girl had no sense of self-preservation.

'Because, you're still here, Bozo! Come on, let's go now! I told those guys to climb into the tree house!'

We had just scampered into the drawing room when we heard the front door crash open. Oh oh, no way we could go into the bedroom and bathroom now. We'd give the game away. More distraction required.

Chick suddenly grabbed me and took me into a clinch much like we had just seen the upstairs couple get into.

'Mmff!' I protested as she planted her lips like Quickfix on mine, our noses mashing together. We clung together, swaying to and fro, just as the men pounded into the room.

As a distraction, it was stunning! Chick had her wits about her all right. The men pulled up short.

'*Abbe*…what the?'

'*Yeh bhi ghar se bhaag rahe hain* (Have they eloped too)?'

'*Aaj kal ke bachche* (Kids nowadays)!' one of the men spat, disgusted.

We parted, blushing furiously and rubbing our noses. Vivek Thakur jerked his chin at us and pointed a rather nasty-looking scissor-like dagger at us. He gave no sign that he recognized us, but the disgust was obvious on his face.

'*Kaha hain?* Where are they?' He barked at the others. '*Dhoondo!* Find them!'

'*Kaun* (Who)?' Chick and I asked simultaneously, sidling between the coffee table and the sofa.

Have to say, Chick had really acted with wisdom. She had not only closed the external bathroom door but had also shoved a large clothes bin in front of it, blocking the door handle from view and indicating that it was not in use. Half the men had already rushed upstairs and now came back, shaking their heads.

'*Samaan hain, par voh nahin* (Their luggage is there but not them)!'

The six men now surrounded us, looking very unpleasant indeed. We'd shifted along the sofa to one end, where the cushions were piled up. Chick's eyes met mine and she nodded ever so faintly. Our arms were down by our side and then our fingers linked. Together, we explored the cushion gaps and then found what we had been looking for—the cold hard metal of a gun butt.

Dr D's silver Smith and Wesson was still stuffed under the cushions. In their panic, the fugitives had forgotten to take it with them. Chick's fingers closed over the butt and she slowly withdrew the gun. I tried taking it from her. She stepped on my foot. I desisted. Wrestling for a loaded gun in this manner was asking for trouble. And we had enough trouble as it was.

'*Ab bhi haat pakad rahe hain; tamasha kar rahe ho* (Are you still holding hands and fooling around)?' Vivek Thankur asked, looking disgusted. '*Sharam nahin aatee* (Aren't you ashamed)? Think of your parents!'

'Now tell us where they've gone or it'll be bad for you!' Ajit Thakur said. 'Quickly!' he yelled.

Chick was holding the gun now, low down, hidden behind her legs and the coffee table. She tensed, readying for action. Both the Thakur goons had guns in their belts too, but were brandishing swords and daggers, as were the others. Then, Vivek Thakur merely nodded at two of the hoods. With horrible grins and bulging eyes, they stepped towards Chick. One of them licked his horrible fish-like lips. I bristled and bunched my fists.

Suddenly, Chick shoved me hard, sideways, on the shoulder, sending me sprawling away from her. The gun was in both her hands and BANG! BANG! BANG! BANG! She fired rapidly, her arms, shoulder and head jerking back violently with the recoil, the flash of the gun bright in the dark room.

The effect was spectacular. The men dived for cover like rats vanishing down the sewers. Two disappeared behind the armchairs, one vanished into the bedroom, and the others, including the Thakur pair, fled to the dining room, and dived under the dining table. They knew exactly how dangerous a gun was in the hands of someone who couldn't shoot. Looking dazed, Chick lowered the smoking gun and then darted towards me.

'Bozo, let's get out!'

Man, was her aim lousy! She missed every single one of them—not a single shot hit its mark! And, this was point-blank range! They must have been not six feet away from us when she started firing. What is it with chicks and firearms man! She could have taken down the whole lot of them. But it also seemed that the damn bullets hadn't gone anywhere else either; there was no whine of ricocheting bullets or 'thwacks' as they embedded themselves in the walls or ceiling, no tinkle and crash of glass shattering. Just, what the heck?

Blanks!

As usual, Dr D had loaded the damn gun with blanks and given it to his guests—so that no one could get hurt!

In seconds, we were out and running. We slammed the front door shut and drew the bolt—hah, it would take them a while to get through that! They might have broken the latch while entering, but the deadbolt and eye outside were fine. Then, the men opened fire too, but the Annex door was solid Burma teak—it could eat bullets.

We were at the base of the tree house in seconds.

I hooted like an owl. Chick simply called out urgently.

'Bhaisahib!'

The ground floor guy peered down, his eyes wide with fear.

'*Neeche aao, jaldi* (Come down quickly)! We have to get out of here! And bring the rucksacks lying there.'

It took them a good three minutes to come down.

'We have to go back to Bedlam House, now!' I said, shouldering my backpack.

From the Annex, we could hear the front door come under major attack. Then, a cry of triumph. Oh crap, they'd discovered the sliding verandah doors. They'd be after us in moments.

'They'll spot us!' Chick and I exchanged glances.

'The hole in the wall!' we said simultaneously. 'We'll go down to the beach!'

I turned to the terrified couples. 'Follow us!'

We ran to the wall and heaved aside the rock blocking the hole. 'Go down, carefully, the steps are steep! And there are thorny plants at the bottom!'

One by one, the fugitives went down.

'Go, Lambu!' I said, even as the men poured into the playground and headed towards the lower garden. Chick ducked, grabbed my hand, and went through, pulling me after her. Have to say, the Thakur duo was sharp. They saw at once that there was no one in the lower garden and looked around, immediately spotting the hole in the base of the wall. There was no way to close it.

We were down at the beach and then some of the stranger things (if you can imagine that) of the night began happening. Without saying a word to each other, both Chick and I made for the creek—we were heading for the formidable Black Diamond rocks beyond.

'Let us head for the tower; we'll be safe there,' we said simultaneously as we entered the creek, ushering our fugitives along. We glanced at each other and splashed across. The tide was again low, and the water about thigh-deep.

We'd forgotten one thing.

On the beach, we'd left a trail of deeply indented footprints in the sand—footprints which our pursuers had no trouble following. We heard some of them howl with pain as they stepped into the spinifex as they got to the bottom, but that didn't deter them for long.

The chase was on.

7

As we splashed across the creek to the other side and headed for the rocks, I turned to see where our pursuers were. The last two were just getting down on the beach and the other four were already following our all-too-clear footprints, one or two hobbling.

'Lambu, you lead, I'll bring up the rear.' I looked at our fugitives. They were all clearly very frightened, possibly in a state of shock.

'We have to climb and go across those rocks and head towards the sea,' I said pointing to the fearsome black massif rising in front of us. 'You'll have to be careful, those rocks are very sharp. Just follow her and do as she does—she knows the best route.' I gulped as two awful doubts struck me.

'Lambu, you got the rope?'

'In the backpack, Bozo, SOP, remember?'

'Good!' I turned to our fugitives. 'Can you climb up and down ropes and swim?' I asked, not very hopefully. They didn't look the type. They stared at each other. Surprisingly, the girls nodded first and the men followed.

'Yes…we used to do that as children on our swings.'

I nodded briefly. '*Karna hoaga*! You'll have to do it now. It's our only way out of here. Come on, let's go. Keep close and be careful of the rocks.'

We began clambering up and across the tumble of sharp rocks that formed the first ridge. It descended into a steep gully.

Thankfully, the moonlight was bright enough and we didn't need the torch (which would have given our location away). Chick went up the first ridge choosing her handholds carefully, but swiftly. The girls and men followed and just before I set off after them, I looked back again. Behind us, our pursuers had crossed the creek and were looking absolutely furious.

It's amazing how fast (and recklessly) you can move when you're being chased. Instinct takes over—Chick leapt over those sharp serrated rocks like a mountain goat and slithered down the slopes and screes sideways, occasionally bracing herself with one hand, with complete confidence. I think it gave our fugitives confidence too, for amazingly, they followed almost perfectly, though with squeals and little screams as the rocks slashed at them. Yes, they were panting, but they kept up pretty well. Occasionally, we gave them a helping hand over really vicious sections, but they managed very well. Fear does that to you, I guess. We splashed through the still, silver-rippled rock pools and then went up the next Black Diamond ridge.

It's also amazing how your pain receptors cut out at such times. It's said that the brain douses the pain nerve endings with endorphins, the same stuff painkillers are made of or something like that, which short circuits the message so the brain doesn't receive any pain signals and enables you to focus on the job at hand. In light shorts and thin cotton T-shirts, neither of us (nor the fugitives) were dressed to take on these shark-toothed rocks, but we did it. We were lucky too that we could duck behind high rocky outcrops and ridges and be out of sight of our pursuers for moments, confusing them a bit. But we heard their yells and curses as the rocks slashed them; they hadn't bargained for this. Have to say, Vivek Thakur was a good tracker. He'd clamber up to a vantage point and scan the rocky outcrops and ridges ahead and also the rocks stretching north. The moonlight bathed everything in eerie silver and black, like crumpled aluminium foil; the shadows were inky black. In white T-shirts and beige and light blue shorts, we were very conspicuous when we moved. Invariably, we'd be spotted as we topped a ridge and scrambled on towards the pincer tip. The chase would resume with shouts of '*Vaha hain*! *Pakdo* (There they are, get them)!' There can be nothing more frightening than a mob—even comprising just six men—chasing you, literally baying for your blood and describing, in very graphic (and biological) language and gruesome detail, exactly what they'd do to you when they caught you.

We slithered down the cheese-grater slope without feeling a thing and at last reached the pincer tip. Chick had the rope out in a jiffy and we tied it around our anchor rock again and flung it over the overhang. It was comforting to know that we'd done this before, even if it was not in the middle of the night. We knew the rope reached the bottom.

'I'll go down first. You send them down after me.' Chick looked at our group—the two couples were standing close together, the men with their arms around the girls' waists. They still looked pretty shell-shocked.

'We have to climb down,' Chick told them succinctly. 'It's about forty feet. And then swim across a channel.' She looked at me. 'I'll give two tugs when I reach down, got it?'

I nodded. 'Copy that!'

The men had seen us clustered there. They were in fact at the top of the cheese-grater slope. The two Thakur guys took out their guns and began firing. We heard the bullets whine and ping and ricochet against the rocks but the range was too great and we were safe. We heard almighty yells of pain as the men began sliding down that serrated slope accompanied by much cursing. It didn't bode well for what they'd do to us if they caught us—they'd make us pay for their pain, that was for sure. They were going to flay us alive. Chick slithered over the cliff edge. Some moments later, she gave me the signal. I turned to one of the girls.

'Please go quickly now and be careful!' She was the girl in jeans and red halter and she nodded her eyes which were bright with both fear and excitement. 'Nitu is down there—it's just a little way down!' She tied up her hair and took a hold of the rope while her partner watched anxiously.

'*Sambhal ke* baby (Be careful baby)!' he said.

'Hold tight, grip the knots with your hands and feet...'

With a squeal she was gone. Her partner anxiously peered over the edge as best as he could but she had disappeared into the darkness. Long, interminable moments later, there were two tugs of the rope. She'd made it!

I beckoned the second girl. 'Your turn...' She smiled.

'Don't worry, Jyoti and I used to do this a lot as children; we used to climb up and down the ropes of our swings and the roots of banyan trees...' She tied her dupatta firmly around her waist, knelt down and took a hold of the rope, and slipped out of sight. After several moments, there were two tugs again. Two down, two to go! I turned to the men.

'Hurry, they've got down the slope and will be hopping mad! You go!' I pointed to the relatively plump fellow. He was looking decidedly nervous. Another shot was fired and this time, a rock a little too close for comfort splintered. 'Go!' He went, with a shout of fright. I just prayed he wouldn't panic and let go of the rope. Some moments later, there were two urgent tugs again. 'Your turn now!' I told the second man. He followed more in a blind panic than anything else. Our pursuers were closing in fast now, cursing fluently as they stumbled over loose rocks or slipped on slime. At last, the fellow was down and I virtually leapt at the rope and swung myself over it. I worked my way down as rapidly as I could, hand over hand, trying not to burn my fingers as I slithered down. At the bottom, Lambu stretched up to catch me. I was coming down far too fast, almost letting go of the rope in my haste.

'Easy there, Bozo!' she grunted, grabbing me around the waist and steadying me. Her hair had come loose and was falling across one side of her face. I looked up at the overhang. Shoot! Vivek Thakur, probably lying flat on his stomach, was staring directly down at me. He was livid, and a tic pulsated hideously, under one bulging eye. A gun appeared in his hand. Chick followed my gaze and shrieked with horror. Bunched together at the bottom of the cliff, we were sitting ducks! There was a bright flash as Vivek Thakur fired. Shocked, we flinched. I felt something whirr past my ear, like when a bumblebee flies too close. I looked up half blinded by the flash; the bugger was drawing bead on me again, carefully. Chick glanced upwards again and with a shriek jerked my head to one side just as he fired a second time. She flinched slightly in reaction to the shot, which really ought to have drilled me clean through the forehead, had she not jerked me violently aside. The bullet bounced off the rocks and whined off into the water. I staggered. She gathered me up in her arms again and held me steady.

'Steady there! You're trembling, Bozo! Are you all right?' she cried in a tone I'd never heard before, her arms tight around me. 'Are you all right, Bozo?' she repeated.

I took a deep breath.

'I'm good, but they're going to come after us! It's like shooting fish in a barrel!'

But in fact, Vivek Thakur had put his gun away and had

begun climbing down the rope, but clumsily. He was obviously not used to doing this kind of thing; sheer rage was driving him. Rather than shooting us to bits, they wanted to get their hands on us—this was personal now.

'Not if I can help it,' Chick snapped. Swiftly, she whipped out the lighter I kept in my rucksack and grabbed at the rope and set it on fire.

'Let's see how he likes this!' she said savagely. The flame hungrily licked its way up the rope, fed by the stiff sea breeze, even as the men, peering over the edge, shouted in alarm and warning. Vivek Thakur gave one horrified look down and began scrambling up as fast as he could. The flame had burned its way halfway up the rope before the men began pulling the rope up. Too bad for them! It would be far too short for them to use.

'Okay, into the water now, swim towards that hole!' We pointed at the black opening of the tunnel across the channel and virtually pushed our fugitives into the water before plunging in after them. 'Swim underwater if you can!' Chick yelled. 'It'll be more difficult for them to shoot at us! Now jump, jump, jump!'

Thankfully, all four of them could swim—and pretty well at that.

We swam across. The water was shoulder-deep now and I could sense that the tide was coming in again. The water was beautifully silvered by the moon—it would have been great for a relaxing swim. Dripping, we trod water at the entrance of the tunnel, and Chick led the way up the steps again, as I brought up the rear. Finally, we reached the base of the tower. Chick flashed the torch up the steps, indicating where we had to go. Our four fugitives stood together, and looked up in amazement.

'*Oopar*, we go up!' I said. I waded back out to the tunnel entrance and looked upwards. From here, you could see the overhang down which we had climbed. Oh damn! A rope was swinging down and Ajit Thakur was gingerly lowering himself down it. At the top, Vivek Thakur waited with his gun ready, ensuring we didn't burn the second rope.

'They've got another rope and are coming after us!' I told Chick tersely. 'The quicker we get up, the better.'

We trudged up round and round the spiral tower steps, and I kept looking out of the gun-slit windows, expecting at any moment to see lights and the faces of those men at the tower base. Silver moonbeams slanted eerily through the slits and occasionally bats would flicker in and out. At the top of the tower, we would be trapped perhaps, but at least we could defend our position by throwing things down at them—rocks and sand. We could have gone around the tower to the cove we had discovered, but would have been completely trapped there too and that too, without the advantage of the high ground.

We stumbled out into the tower. It was all silver and black and rustling with restless bats funneling in and out. All of us were out of breath. We sat on the plinth and looked at each other, trying to get our breath back.

The girl in the jeans and the red halter, Jyoti, I think she was, looked at us and smiled. 'Thank you ji,' she said softly. 'Thank you for helping us escape.'

'They were going to kill us all,' the second girl said.

The men remained quiet and looked at each other. I shook my head. I knew we hadn't gotten away just yet.

'Who are they?' Chick asked.

'Papa and our Uncle,' the girls said together. 'We are sisters.'

'I'm Jyoti and she's Ujjala,' the girl in jeans said. 'We...we eloped and married against the wishes of our family...and they said we had brought shame and dishonour to the family name.

They had got us engaged to...others—uncouth, crude men.' She made a disgusted face. 'Now they want to kill us. Mrs Dubash and the doctor sahib helped us escape and have arranged our departure for America.' They were holding the hands of their husbands as they spoke. The men just nodded.

'We're still not entirely safe,' I said gruffly. 'Once they come down, they'll see the tunnel entrance and know where we are. The tide is still low enough so the tunnel entrance will be exposed.'

The girls smiled wanly. 'The other men might not want to come up here,' Ujjala said softly. 'They'll think the place is haunted. They're all very superstitious. The men they've brought are labourers from our farm, very scared of the supernatural. This place is spooky. They don't like bats. They've probably never seen the sea either.'

It was spooky but cool up in the tower, a bit chilly though as our clothes were wet and clingy. I looked around, hoping to find rocks and stones which, we could—if it came to that—fling down at our pursuers if they came up the tower stairs. There were none big enough to be a deterrent, which was surprising—just scrunchy, silvery dry sand and some pebbles.

'Let me see what they are doing,' I said and slipped back into the tower. There was no one at the base. I slipped down to the first gun-slit window facing the pincer spur and looked out. Oh, oh! They had made it to the bottom of the cliff and were looking around, puzzled. They didn't seem to know where we'd gone. They stared at the water, obviously wondering if we had dared to swim through the channel into the open sea. I went back up and out into the moonlight.

'Looks like we're okay for the time being,' I told the others. 'They don't know where we've gone. They haven't seen the tunnel entrance. Even better, the tide is coming in, so hopefully, it will soon cover the entrance completely.'

Chick was sitting beside the two girls. She had gone into her nosy parker mode.

'How did you learn about Mridula Autny's NGO?' she asked them.

Ujjala smiled. 'Oh, it is well-known in our college. They actually helped a friend of ours settle in New Zealand with her boyfriend. It's like a helpline!'

'And you both...and they both...got married secretly?' Oh yes, this was right up Chick's alley.

'Yes. We met in medical college; our parents did not approve at all. In fact, we had to fight tooth and nail just to go to college. So we met, how do you say, clandestinely, for three years and then Papa said we had to get married and forget about all this medicine rubbish.'

The other girl chipped in. 'Then, the balloon sort of went up, because they found out about us... They locked us up at home... and tried to get us engaged to these louts... But we had been in touch with Mridula ma'am much before that and she had told us to apply for US visas if we could, and to keep our passports with us at all times. We managed to do that...' She swallowed as her eyes filled up. 'But papa and thaiyaji sent goondas after Jai and Lokeshbhai who beat them up and told them never to come near us again or they'd throw acid on us and blame them.'

'What happened then?' Chick was agog. Both the girls smiled and looked adoringly at their husbands, sitting stoically side-by-side.

'They both came! We managed to smuggle out a message saying we would be outside this sari shop in Delhi on one particular day at around 4 p.m. because mama was taking us wedding shopping that day. We were to get engaged the next evening. We both had our passports with us. So we stood outside the shop, with all these bags in our hands, pretending to argue about where to go next, when they rode up on their bikes and we just climbed on behind them and zoomed off, bags and all, before mama and thaiyiji knew what was happening. The boys had also been in touch with Mridula ma'am and Dubash sir who had given them an address and we stayed there for a few days. The people in the house, who were friends of the Dubashes, did more shopping for us—clothes and things because we'd come away with only our shopping bags. They also called a priest and got us married! Later, we caught a train to Mumbai. But papa and thaiya got wind of it somehow and we think they followed us with their men.' Her eyebrows shot up. 'Well they must have—they're here now,' she added. Their husbands looked on quietly.

'What about you two?' Ujjala suddenly asked with a smile. 'You have also taken sanctuary with the Dubashes and are running away together?'

'But you are so very young! Like Romeo and Juliet almost!' They giggled.

'Did you know Romeo was only 16 and Juliet 14 when they fell in love? They started early in those days!'

I went scarlet and Chick grinned and shook her head.

'No, no, nothing like that. We've lived here all our lives—our parents are tenants of the Dubashes and we live in the big house.' She rolled her eyes. 'Of course, Dr D teases him a lot though.'

I got to my feet and went back into the tower. Oh crap! Harsh voices echoed up from the bottom of the tower. The men had entered the base of the tower. I hurried back.

'They've discovered the tunnel entrance and are now at the bottom. We'll have to do something to defend ourselves. They'll be up in no time at all!'

It was then that the strange thing happened to Chick and me for the second time that night. We exchanged glances and walked into the little guardhouse almost like zombies.

'Are you thinking what I'm thinking?' Chick murmured, sotto voce. I glanced at her. Her inky blue-black cascading hair, outlining her grave oval face, made her look really beautiful. I nodded briefly.

'I guess! Let's get to work.'

Our fugitives peered in from the doorway—there were shrieks and muffled shouts and they backed out hastily when they saw what we were doing.

Chick looked around and went out to them. 'Can I borrow your dupatta, please?' she asked Ujjala.

Loud, rough voices echoed up the tower from the base. I peered over the edge. Oh, hell, the men were gathered around at the bottom. They were holding powerful torches in their hands, flashing them upwards and peering up in astonishment. Vivek and Ajit Thakur stared at the steps, alas, still gleaming with puddles of water that had formed as it dripped off us while we had climbed up.

'They've gone up!' he shouted. 'Come on, we've got them now! *Kaat kaat ke tanga denge* (We'll cut them up and hang them)!' There was a brief argument and then they started up the steps, followed albeit a little reluctantly by the four others, who were still staring up at the gaunt granite walls, their eyes wide with apprehension.

I rushed back to the guardhouse where Chick had nearly completed our task. Our fugitives were staring at us as if we had gone crazy, but then Jyoti and Ujjala smiled tightly and began to help. Their husbands hovered uneasily in the background.

The idea that had struck Chick and me simultaneously again was simple—we'd exhume Romeo and Juliet, and fling their bones at our pursuers, hopefully spooking them enough to give up the chase. Being brained by a grinning skull falling through a dark tower, lit by slivers of silver moonlight as if by a stroboscope could be pretty disconcerting, I imagined. The problem was that we couldn't pry loose the skeletons from one another! It was like they were fused together. The skulls sat firm on the neck vertebrae, each one's forehead fused to the other's and the arms stuck fast on the shoulders and in their sockets. Each skeleton was attached to the other as if they had fossilized together. They were a single entity. Or what, I thought with a wry grin, we would today call an 'item'. Nor did the bones of the arms or legs or fingers and toes come apart—they were like cemented together. Talk about rigor mortis man!

'Bozo!' Chick whispered in awe. 'That's what you call true love! Even death hasn't done them apart. We'll have to lift them out together, embracing as they have been for so many centuries.'

'And then...?'

'Yes, we'll have to!' There were tears in Chick's eyes.

'It's okay Chick, what has to be done, has to be done! It's our only hope.' She gave me a real strange look when I said that, and for a moment, I wondered why.

You should have seen the faces of the fugitives when we struggled through the guardhouse door carrying Romeo and Juliet still in a clinch between us. They nearly fainted.

'We're going to spook them with these,' I said tersely.

'Very appropriately!' Chick added.

Just then, my phone rang. Aslam!

'Boss, I have six missed calls from you...'

Tersely, I told him what had happened.

'Warn the Dubashes and come to the tower pronto in The Bedlam! We need backup!'

'Roger that!'

'Give me the phone!' Chick suddenly said and grabbed it. She moved away a little distance and spoke in a low urgent tone.

'Wh…what was that?'

'Nothing. I wanted to know how Cushion was.' She shrugged. Girls! We were in the middle of a do-or-die situation and she was asking about her dog! Then, she went back to the skeletons, and with the help of the girls, put the dupatta through the shoulder bones of Romeo and Juliet, stringing them together as it were—not that they were in any danger of coming apart. Holding the edges of the dupatta at each end and moving apart, we asked the girls to gently push the tragic lovers over the edge, so they hung in space as it were. Their husbands seemed too psyched to be of any help. With a little effort, the girls got Romeo and Juliet over the rim and we held on to the dupatta ends, suspending them in mid-air, looking macabre as hell, and still kissing!

The men were climbing up; the Thakur pair ahead of the others, panting heavily. They'd stop from time to time and urge the others to hurry. Then, one of the laggards suddenly gave a shout.

'*Arre baap re, dekho* (Oh God, look)!'

It must have been quite a sight—two skeletons in a tight clinch, hanging in black space, lit ghoulishly by the light of the torches and silver moonbeams as bats danced and flickered around them. They couldn't see Chick or me because we were now lying flat on the plinth hanging on to the dupatta ends, out of their line of sight.

Vivek and Ajit Thakur, now perhaps just twenty feet below us, stopped and whipped out their guns.

And then yet again, Lambu and I reacted in the same way, and with no conscious decision really. We just knew what we had to do. We scrambled to our knees and swung Romeo and Juliet to and fro, till we had a good momentum going.

'On the count of three, Bozo!' Chick grunted. 'Three two one—heave!' With a mighty effort, we let them go.

Just as those two bastards raised their revolvers and fired. Again, I heard the bumblebee whir of the bullet past my ear and Chick squealed and flinched.

But I swear, those skeletons took matters into their own hands thereafter. In slow-motion, they somersaulted in mid-air and headed, like smart bombs, straight for Vivek and Ajit Thakur now standing stock still as if hypnotized, their guns in their hands. Suddenly, with a hideous flurry, a large family of bats, spooked by the gunshots perhaps, fluttered desperately past the men and up the tower and poured into the night sky.

I can tell you, you'd be pretty spooked if you were brained by a pair of smooching moonlit skeletons somersaulting on top of you from a height of twenty feet or so, with bats fluttering around your ears at the same time.

'Their final act of love!' Chick declaimed, clutching my hand, as the skeletons crashed right into Vivek and Ajit Thakur and finally shattered almost explosively. The guns were knocked out of the men's nerveless hands and fell into the pool at the bottom of the tower.

'Eternal love's revenge!' Chick said, but she was suddenly looking very pale. The two skulls, still seemingly fused together like those of Siamese twins, bounced down the stairs ghoulishly, shedding teeth, heading straight towards the other four guys who nearly pushed each other off the steps in their panic to get out of their way and go back down. It was raining bones down the tower. The rib cages of the poor dead lovers, also still tangled together, bounced down behind the skulls, like ancient fossilized tumbleweed, Ujjala's dupatta still fluttering macabrely around their shoulders, as it would have been had Juliet been wearing it. Those men freaked. Vivek and Ajit, now disarmed and disoriented, lay stunned and groggy on the stairs, holding their heads, while their gang turned and fled down the steps, screaming, '*Bhoot, bhoot, bachao, bachao* (Ghosts! Ghosts)! *Bhago, bhago* (Run, run)!' Then, some of the bats crapped straight into Vivek's eye for he suddenly clutched his face with his hands and gabbled:

'*Andha kar diya* (It has blinded me)!'

It was the last straw as far as the enemy was concerned. Ajit took his brother by the hand and began leading him down the steps; he was shaking with fear.

Suddenly, Chick, who was right next to me, sort of swayed sideways towards me. I glanced at her—she was white as a sheet. She put her hand to her right side and then her ear and it came out glistening dark red. Dark red, with blood. Then, she staggered against me.

'Chick, you've been shot!' I gasped, struggling to hold her up as she stared at her hand uncomprehendingly. 'One of the shots must have hit you!' She just nodded. 'Let me see! Come on sit down here, let me get the first-aid!' Oblivious to everything else, I gently sat her down on the plinth.

'Raise your arms: I have to take the T-shirt off.' She obeyed, her eyes widening ever so slightly. I pulled the T-shirt over her head. Oh God! It was a mess! The bullet had gouged a furrow across her ribs; ripping through her slip; blood was flowing down her side. It had also sheared off a bit of the lobe of her ear. 'I'll have to take the slip off too, Chick!' I said, slipping the straps off her shoulders. Again, she just nodded quietly. She was very pale (with loss of blood I guessed, almost panicking at the thought).

'Sit down…here, let me get the first-aid!' I took the first-aid kit out of my backpack (thank god for SOP) and opened it, glancing tensely at her. She'd closed her eyes—was she beginning to lose consciousness?

'Lambu, are you okay? Nitu, do you read me?' I patted her cheek gently. 'Say something, open your eyes! Hang in there, Chick!'

Her eyes flickered open.

'Look at me! Stay awake! Stay with me!'

Suddenly, her face became all blurry and glimmery. For a second, I wondered what was happening, and then furiously rubbed away the tears that had flooded my eyes and gulped down the massive frog in my throat. She was looking at me with her grave, glinting eyes.

'Chick, you'll be fine!' I said hoarsely. 'You'd better be fine,' I thought; what the heck would I do without you? 'I have you now!' I held her head tightly against my chest. 'There, I got you now, Chick, I got you! You'll be fine—you're with me!' Man, if she were to die at least it would be in my arms—someone she'd known all her life. It might be of some comfort to her. But not to me. She couldn't die! She just couldn't. He eyes closed gently again and she sighed.

'You can't die, Chick! Not here, not now, not ever!' I blurted brokenly. I bent over her and kissed her blindly all over her face. 'Please, Chick, wake up, you've got to wake up!' Her eyes flickered open and scanned my face wonderingly. Slowly, she raised a hand and wiped a stubborn tear still running down my cheek and then her arms went around me and she kissed me.

'Thanks, Bozo! I'm feeling better now,' she whispered hoarsely, her cheek against mine. 'It was just a spell of dizziness; I must have fainted.' I frowned. Was that a sly smile at the edges of her mouth? Had she made a Mickey of me again? Those damn books! But...

Then Jyoti and Ujjala stepped forward swiftly. Jyoti quickly examined the first-aid kit and Ujjala began looking at Chick's ear and ribs. The men hovered in the background, looking at the ground because Chick had no top on.

'*Hum karenge*...we'll do it,' Jyoti said, smiling at me. 'We're doctors—all four of us!'

Man, was that a relief or what! Not one, but four doctors. Briskly, Ujjala tied up Chick's hair into a topknot and began taking stuff out of the first-aid kit.

'Thank you,' Chick whispered, still looking terribly pale.

'Chick, you'll be fine,' I said, 'See, I got four doctors to tend to you! I take care of what's mine! What do you think, eh?'

'Always, Bozo!'

I turned to the girls. 'She will be okay, won't she?' I asked hoarsely. 'She's not dying or anything, is she?'

They smiled and Jyoti patted my hand. 'She's got a shallow flesh wound, that's all; and her ear lobe might need a few small stitches. She'll be fine. Don't worry! Your girlfriend will be fine. She's just a bit shocked but anyone would be after being shot at.'

'Oh! Are you sure?'

'Yes! Don't worry! We'll look after her.' I looked at Chick gulping with relief.

'Where are those men?' she asked, wincing, as the girls applied antiseptic and gently began cleaning and bandaging her ear and ribs.

'Dunno...I'd better check! We're out of bones...I mean ammo now...' I peered over the wall. There was no one on the steps or at the base of the tower. They had gone!

Not quite though. Suddenly, I heard shouts and excited voices and the sounds of a scuffle. A dog—a very familiar dog—yapped. And there, at the base of the tower, flashing torches up towards the top, was Aslam along with Dr Dubash, Mridula Aunty, Cushion and Night and three cops. They stared astounded at the bones of poor Romeo and Juliet scattered around on the ground and glimmering at them from the bottom of the pool.

'Are you up there, Nitu?' Dr Dubash bellowed. 'Are you kids all right?'

I gulped. Oh shit, now I'd have to face him—whom I had so royally betrayed, even if I had tried to warn him off.

'Yes, we're all here. We're good,' I replied, looking over the edge. 'Nitu's been shot in the ear and ribs but she's okay now...'

He pounded up the steps on the double, followed by the others.

We were finally escorted back to the base of the tower; Chick sandwiched between Dr D and Mridula Aunty. Jyoti and Ujjala had slipped on her T shirt after they had bandaged her ribs. I followed, along with the two husbands, as Aslam carried a squirming Cactus in his arms. The Lily of the West was docked in the cove. Two more cops, guarded Vivek and Ajit Thakur, who were handcuffed and who glared lividly as we emerged. Of the other four guys there was no sign.

'They shot at us twice!' I said, 'They shot Nitu and me at nearly point-blank range!'

'Then, they're in for an attempt to murder,' Dr D said grimly, as he and Mridula Aunty made Chick lie down on one of the bunks in the cabin.

Jyoti, Ujjala and their husbands averted their eyes from the Thakurs and quietly ducked into the cabin too. Dr D quickly examined Chick's ear (and ribs), clicked his fingers near it and asked her if she could hear.

'Yes, Uncle, I can hear fine,' she said. He leant forward and whispered something to her, glancing slyly at me. And man, Chick blushed!

I sat at the foot of her bunk just staring at her while Aslam took Cactus and went outside. I heard the engines start and the boat began to move.

It was nearing five o'clock and there was the faintest glimmer of orange in the east as we sailed across the lagoon. At the jetty, an interesting sight met our eyes. The fishing boat, which the intruders had used, was moored there, with two cops on board. They had apparently found the fisherman, whose boat it was, gagged and tied up in the tiny cabin.

'There were four more men,' I told Dr D, not daring to look him in the eye. 'They've escaped.'

'Not quite yet,' he replied with a sardonic grin. 'Look, there they are!' He pointed down the beach towards the creek. The four hoodlums had just come across it and were running down the beach towards the jetty. What they hadn't seen was the entire canine corps lined up near the fishing boat, waiting for orders.

'*Chodo*! Release them!' the cop in charge shouted as Mridula Aunty waved and nodded. Joyfully, the German shepherds raced after their quarry.

It was over.

Now, all that was left was the court martial I (and Chick and Aslam) would have to face about this whole affair.

8

'So let me get this straight,' Dr D said as we sat before him and Inspector Borkar (who was an old friend of the Dubashes and whose German shepherd aunty had trained) in his clinic later that morning. Jyoti, Ujjala and their husbands had returned to the Annex after giving their statements to the police. Dr D was addressing Chick. Earlier, I had stood by as Dr D had stitched up and dressed her shot-up ear and ribs properly. She was pretty pale and I tried not to show how woozy I felt as I gripped her hand to reassure her that I was with my team even when everything was all right; she squeezed it back tightly. I had then gone home and showered and changed before returning to the Dubashes. Chick was now back in her favourite olive green skirt and a floppy blouse, still looking a bit pale. Our parents would be returning in the afternoon.

'You say you were standing out in the verandah last night and saw the intruders' boat come in and thought they were terrorists...' Dr D went on. Chick nodded. I let her do all the talking; chicks were better at that sort of thing and man, after what had happened to her, I didn't trust myself talking.

'Yes,' she said, 'at first, that's what I thought, what with the Mumbai attacks and all. So, I told Bozo and he got very excited. But then, we recognized those two Thakur men—who had brought the German shepherd puppies and had asked us all sorts of questions about Jyoti and Ujjala and their husbands.'

'Who you three made friends with and made brownies for, I believe,' Mridula Aunty said, smiling faintly. 'That's what those girls told us!'

'Yes...and Jyoti and Ujjala told us how they'd eloped and that their families were after them...and how you and Uncle had helped them. And then, when the men turned up in the boat, well, Bozo here, believe it or not, put two and two together and realized that these fellows were not terrorists but probably angry family members wanting to harm them. He said they didn't have any RPG thingies with them or something, which terrorists normally carry.'

I stared at her astounded. What the heck was she up to, concocting this complete cock-and-bull story? And such a flimsy one at that! Mridula Aunty only had to find out that the two girls had only told us what had happened when we were up in the tower, not when we had brought them the brownies—that would let all the cats out of the bag. I glanced at Chick again, but her hair, loose once more, obscured her face. She glanced briefly at me and then away. I cleared my throat, but Dr D ignored me. Inspector Borkar took down notes, which worried me a bit.

'So why didn't you wake us up, dear?' Dr D asked her pointedly.

Chick smiled sheepishly and shrugged. 'Uncle, I guess, we got too excited. We had to rush off and warn them at the Annex that these fellows were after them.'

'Umm...do you know anything about this strange e-mail that was lying in my inbox this morning? From a "Well-wisher" it says...' Again, he looked at Chick.

She blushed. 'Umm...Uncle, that was me too,' she admitted. 'You see, when I first saw the boat last night and thought it was a terrorist attack, I thought that...that...you had mistakenly of course, sheltered more of them, um...Jyoti and Ujjala and their husbands at the Annex...thinking that they were...err...genuine honeymooners escaping from their families.... But...then...then I remembered your gun that I saw in the Annex when we took them the brownies...and wondered why you would give it to them ...and the terrorist suspicion arose again. I thought that Jyoti and Ujjala had sold us a big romantic cover-up story. But then, Bozo kept insisting that these guys looked like thugs not commandoes, and that even if it was true that they were terrorists after all and... and that you were involved we should warn you because everyone deserves a second chance... So, that's what I did then...sent you the message. Um...just in case they were terrorists after all....' She looked sheepishly at the ground and squirmed—even if not very convincingly. My head spun as I tried figuring out exactly what was going on. One thing I knew and I was gobsmacked at it—Chick had taken the rap for me! 100 per cent.

The question was: Why?

'Hmm... I see,' Dr D said dryly, nodding, a twinkle deep in his eye as he glanced at both of us and at Inspector Borkar.

'So...Uncle, why did you give them your Smith and Wesson and load it with blanks?' Chick asked.

'To reassure them! They were terrified of their families, so I gave it to them... I loaded it with blanks to make sure they didn't start anything we would all regret... young people in love can do very silly things.' He frowned, 'but how did you know it was loaded with blanks?'

'I fired it at the men,' Chick said simply. 'They had cornered us!'

'In self-defence,' I added quickly. 'They had knives and daggers and guns too.'

'Hmm... See, that's also why I had loaded it with blanks. Otherwise you would have cleaned out the whole bunch. No great loss, but still…it would have complicated matters considerably.'

Mridula Aunty smiled. 'I think we owe you an explanation too,' she said. 'You see dears, when the doctor and I got married, my parents too were very against it, and we had to…well, elope just like Jyoti and Ujjala. My parents were unfortunately very old-fashioned and rigid and made things very difficult for us and disinherited me. But we came through it all. Uncle had this lovely house and farm, so we came here and decided to help other couples who faced similar problems. That's what my NGO really does. Jyoti and Ujjala met their husbands in medical college. They're solid, decent boys but their parents were too proud and stupid to allow them to choose their own partners. We've helped several such couples.' She sighed, 'Sometimes, of course, it doesn't work out, but many times it does, and anyway, it's always worth a shot!'

'Did you really throw skeletons of lovers at those fellows?' Dr D chortled. 'You kids are something else, really!'

'Yes, we had found them buried in the tower earlier…and thought we'd psyche the fellows. There was nothing else we could do!'

'But Uncle, those skeletons sort of homed in on those guys like guided missiles,' Chick said earnestly. 'It was really weird!'

So she had noticed it too: How the somersaulting skeletons had seemingly deliberately headed straight for the Thakur fellows.

'Well, we have a small reward for the two of you,' Dr D went on as Mridula Aunty got up and went into the 'dogs-cum-children's' waiting room. She came back with the two wriggling German shepherd pups.

'These are for you,' she smiled, 'I think you deserve them! Bobby and Tommy! You can continue with their training classes at the earliest. They'll be complimentary.'

Apparently, Jyoti and Ujjala's father had suspected that the

Dubashes had had something to do with helping their daughters escape and had bought the puppies just to enable them easy access to Bedlam House. It was easier than they thought, because they had found the two of us to help them. We had royally played into their hands.

Have to say, the cops were very thorough about checking out our story. Inspector Borkar listened to Chick quietly and then said that they'd require verification of what she'd told them, just to be sure everything fit. We had to take them to the Annex, show them the smashed door, where the showdown had taken place; the Smith and Wesson was still under the sofa where Chick had kicked it after firing it in vain. We showed them the way down the cliff steps, the creek and how we had crossed the shark-toothed Black Diamond Rocks. They followed me, (Chick was not allowed strenuous physical activity and stayed back after we'd shown them the Annex) cursing all the way as the rocks, and especially the cheese-grater, slashed them. Then, I showed them the overhang—the men's rope still hung there (along with our charred one). They were a bit loath to follow me down—only one guy was game enough. So I climbed down the cliff and pointed at the tunnel entrance across the channel. By now, they were quite impressed by my physical prowess and seemed less sceptical. They went around by boat again and gathered up the scattered bones of Romeo and Juliet from the base. The skulls, lying at the bottom of the pool, were still fused together forehead-to-forehead, and still kissing, even if several teeth were now missing. They left them there—they were satisfied. No one likes interrupting kissing couples, especially if they've been at it for hundreds of years!

'All the men will be charged with attempt to kidnap and murder,' Inspector Borkar told us. 'They tried to kill you children and their own daughters. The four men have sung like canaries;

you spooked the heck out of them. You did very well.' His eyes bore into me. 'Next time, anything like this happens you tell Dr Dubash or come to us straightaway. Don't try and do anything on your own—you've seen what can happen.' Shit, he seemed to be saying, 'I know exactly what happened; that girl is covering for you!' He was no dumb bunny.

'Yes, sir,' I said quietly.

Chick and I met at the tree house later that afternoon; she climbed up in spite of her ribs. She was like that, as you know by now. I looked at her.

'So why did you tell Dr D and the inspector that cock-and-bull story?' I asked.

'Wasn't a cock-and-bull story! What are you talking about?'

'You took the rap, Chick. When it was my fault! I suspected Dr D from the start, not you!'

'Well, you were man enough to admit you were wrong when the truth came out. And you were consumed with guilt because you thought you were betraying both him and the country!'

'It's odd; Dr D and the Inspector didn't ask me a single question. He just spoke to you!'

'Probably because he knew he'd get clearer answers from me than you, Bozo,' she replied, the familiar glint back in her eyes.

'Oh, sure...'

But it was bothering me; and a lot. I just had to clear the air. That evening, as Dr D ushered out his last patient, I rang the clinic door. Sophia opened it.

'Hello dear...you're not feeling well?'

'Is Dr D in?' I asked, 'I'd like to see him.'

'Come this way!'

He was scrolling up and down on his computer and looked up as I entered.

'Hello, *beta*...everything all right?'

'Umm...yes, no...I don't know...' I gulped. 'Dr D, what... what Nitu told you this morning...'

He came over to me and put his arm around my shoulders, his eyes twinkling.

'I know. She's a fine girl, *beta*, a really fine girl... Don't you think so?'

'Yes, yes of course...but...'

'Yes, I know, it can be very confusing...at your age...'

'It's not....'

'I know she teases you a lot, but...remember that song...'

'But...'

'I think she feels about you the way you feel about her, *beta*,' he said, 'and that's wonderful, don't you think?'

'Um...yes, I guess!' I went red, but persisted. 'But those things she told you...about what happened...they...they weren't exactly um...like that or...true...'

He nodded. 'I know, *beta*. No one should be caught between the kind of rock and a hard place like you were. So should we conclude this matter now?'

'Okay, Uncle, and thanks!'

He gave me a hug and saw me out as he always does. 'She's worth more than her weight in gold, *beta*,' he said seriously. I just nodded and fled.

I went down to the beach where I met Aslam.

'Hi,' he complained, 'you guys have all the fun and I get stuck with the piano!' He looked at me. 'That Nitu, she really digs you, man!'

'What are you talking about?'

'This morning, when I called, she spoke to me. She told me what to tell Dr D—that it was all her idea and that he should believe her and not listen to anything you might say. She was covering for you man, big time. She said she knew that Dr D would probably guess that it was all your doing, but he should pretend not to know and only question her.'

'Oh!'

He grinned. 'So you and her...?'

'We're cool, that's it. She saved my life when that bugger fired at me. Shoved my head out of the way.'

He nodded. 'I guess. She's like that only. Okay, I have to go. Back to the piano! Thank god, only a week left before the exam. Then I'll be free!' He walked off.

That evening, Chick came down the garden steps to the beach with all the four dogs. I'd been mooching about on the sand, kicking shells around.

'I've been looking for you everywhere, Bozo!' she complained as she came up to me. 'Have you been running away from me?'

'What? Of course not! You could have rung! How're your ribs and ear?'

'I'll live!'

'Is it painful?'

'Stiff. I have to be careful while sleeping.'

'All that blood—it really freaked me out, I tell you!'

'Sorry about that, Bozo; when you get shot, you bleed.' She looked at me. I shrugged.

'I guess.'

'You were good back there. Some of those things you said when you discovered I'd been shot...were so...so um...un-Bozo-like! Sweet, you know.'

'What things?'

'I won't embarrass you by repeating them, but they were really sweet!'

'Uh...really?' I shrugged. 'Well you were...we were both pretty badly freaked out, so stuff gets said.'

'I guess! Say, like to go back to the tower again?'

'You can't do all that climbing, remember?'

'We can take The Bedlam to the cove!'

So that's what we did after leaving the dogs with poor Mridula Aunty.

We sat by the pool at the bottom of the tower, looking at the skulls, still glimmering at the bottom, still kissing. The cops hadn't dared to touch them!

'Wow! Even that fall and rolling down all those steps hasn't separated them,' Chick said, awe in her voice.

'The bones must have fused; like being welded together.'

'You know what?' Chick said looking at me with a strange quirky smile on her face.

'What?'

'That's what you really call, living "happily ever after"!'

'Uh huh! I suppose.'

'Like this,' she said huskily and wrapped her arms around me and kissed me right on the lips. She drew back at last, and looked at me gravely. 'And now Bozo, you have to braid my hair again, so get on with it!'

And this time, after I had finished, she rested her head against my chest again and left it there. Then, she caught my hands and put them around her waist and rested her cheek against mine.

'You read too much mush, Chick!' I told her in her unshot ear. 'And it's having a disastrous effect on you! Just look at you! Not what I trained you for!'

'Not what you trained me for?' The withering sarcasm and gimlet look were back! I nodded briefly.

'Ya, just look at you...tsk, tsk!'

'I think...' she said slowly, 'I think that at this moment, it's having the same effect on you too, in a very big way.'

'It makes you feel you need a guy to look after you.'

'Bozo!'

'Don't worry! I'll look after you; just part of the job description, you know; no hassle. But for *you*...I mean you're Chick after all...a real tough cookie...and look what it's done to you! Made you a marshmallow! You need looking after—someone to braid your hair!'

'Tough cookie, Bozo? I'll marshmallow you in a minute!'

'Hey, Chick, cool it!'

'You cool it!' she said, shoving me headlong into the pool. 'You know something? You already are one—the biggest sweetest one I know!'

Acknowledgements

Thanks to Aparna for clearing the clutter.

www.ingramcontent.com/pod-product-compliance
Lightning Source LLC
Chambersburg PA
CBHW050347030726
47503CB00008B/2664